THE FANTASY OF LOVE:
THE BROKEN MIRROR

The Fantasy of Love:
The Broken Mirror

Tshombe

TS Amen Publishing
2018

First Printing: 2011

ISBN 978-1-7321857-0-8

TS Amen Publishing
490 Lake Park Avenue, 10824
Oakland, CA 94610

www.tsamenpublishing.com

Dedication

This book is dedicated in loving memory to Shakir Stewart, my big cousin. You were and always will be larger than life. I haven't forgotten your advice. We all miss you a lot. I love you Fam!

Introduction

This is the first book in the *Fantasy of Love* series. In this book you will read three individual stories from the perspective of those in love with a young lady born under a curse called The Broken Mirror. The reason for the curse and how it will be broken will unfold through the details of each story. For those who have been in love, are in love, seek to be in love, or those who wish to never be in love again, this book has been created for you.

Please keep in mind that no one owns love and sharing love with someone you choose is a luxury, not a right. Enjoy the moments you reflect love and avoid holding love alone, because that is the curse of the broken mirror.

Part One
Family Strangers

She sat watching the man, knowing he was taking his last breath. Though each gasp was more troubled than the last, it would be a while before the poison stopped his heart. The room in disarray looked as though it had been abandoned to vagrants. The two of them and the mess they had created were the only responsible parties here. A lamp on its side offered the only light. The hostess was not concerned with fixing decor in this place she once called home. Her eyes glimmered in the dim light as she surveyed her surroundings; stimulated by the remnants of the poisoned man's struggle, the residence had never looked more beautiful.

She moved slowly, circling the chair holding her prey. She peered at his wrists and ankles bound tightly by her rope, crimson dripping to the floor. Smiling approvingly, she sat down in front of him examining the effects of her handiwork: the terror in his expression, his fear that she may bring more broken glass to his skin. In this room the man recognized hell as the demon before him spoke.

"You're probably wondering why I've done this, but I'm sure if you put the pieces together the picture to this puzzle should be quite clear. You know what? I'm being very rude. Where are my manners? My name, as you know, is Cassandra and I will be your hostess for your last night of life. We only have a little time, so let me begin."

She poured a glass of wine, took a sip, and laughed.

"You know what, Charles? This apartment is probably the best place I've ever lived in. Unlike the fancy homes you're accustomed to, I've always been one step above no home at all. Did your parents raise you?" She asked as if he was going to answer back.

"Well, I wouldn't know what that's like. My parents got rid of me as soon as I was born. Can you imagine what that must be like? Can you imagine the people who created you not even wanting to be bothered with caring for you? Can you imagine that? I was unloved the day I was born. I was never told how I came into foster care and by the time I was old enough to ask, nobody knew. Maybe they just didn't care, but the fact remains I never found out. You know, a lady told me once that it really didn't matter how or why I was where I was. I was there and that's all I needed to know. I'm sure you can see why I hated her answer. I bounced around from group home to group home and all this bitch could tell me is that I'm there! I guess she thought I didn't know. They treated us as if we were all stupid anyway. I guess in her mind, I needed to be reminded.

"You know what my very first memory is? You'll never guess! This has got to be something everyone remembers. I must have been six-years-old. It was a trip to the doctor's office. I was so happy, and I can't remember why; because happy thoughts are something that just didn't happen for me that often. Well, I'm in the doctor's office eating candy and the woman who brought me down there is crying. It didn't really bother me. I guess even then I had stopped crying. People crying was something you got used to in the foster care system. So, as I'm watching this woman crying she's walking towards me saying, 'Who touched you? 'Who touched you?' Over and over again. All I wanted was more candy. I didn't answer her. To tell you the truth I can't remember who hadn't touch me. The older boys were always sneaking around at night. That's sad huh? I don't even remember the first time I was intimate with someone. I thought it was normal to play with boys like that. I really thought that everyone my age played like that. Silly me! Finally, after catching me playing inappropriately, my first-grade teacher told me that wasn't the case. I don't remember what I said, but I know I went to another foster home that same day.

"You know what? I think that's the first day I began to feel bad about who I was. Can you imagine a six-year-old child ashamed of who she is? That's got to be the worst thing on earth. So now, I did what most do when they feel like that. I shut myself out from the world. I refused to let anyone into my life because people in my life only made me feel worse.

"At school, I became the kid who sat by herself. Other kids tried to be my friend, but I wouldn't even talk to them. Some even tried to tease me out of my shell, but all that did was drive me further into my fortress. I watched them play, wondering if just one of them was like me; if just one of them had ever felt what it's like not to be loved. Just one! At the end of those days, their parents would pick them up and I would catch the bus home with the grownups. Then one day as if by magic, this girl showed up at school. She was the new kid, so nobody played with her. During lunch, she came and sat next to me on my bench, but I didn't say a word to her. I just stared. She had really pretty eyes that seemed to talk to me when I looked at her. They seemed to say, 'I'm just like you.' But that was impossible, you know! At that time in my life I thought there couldn't be anyone on earth who was like me. As the lunch break went on, I became fascinated by this new, powerful presence in my world. I watched her when she wasn't looking, fearful of those beautiful, talking eyes. I studied her face, hands, hair, and her clothes without her noticing. I consumed every inch of her and by the end of the day, I was in love.

"As usual, I watched the rest of the kids after school get picked up by their parents, but this time it was different. Someone else stayed behind with me: the girl with the beautiful, talking eyes. She stood away from me as if to mirror me or something. She wouldn't look at me when I looked at her, but when I turned away I could feel her watching just as I had done with her earlier. I tried to catch her eye, but she always looked away. It became a game for us to take turns studying each other while the other looked away. Does that game sound familiar, Charles? Is that something you've played before while seducing your conquests? I bet you have."

She tossed a small cup of rubbing alcohol in his face causing him to scream. She laughed, enjoying his misery.

"You listen to me while I'm talking to you or I will cut you in worse places and clean your wounds with more of what was in that cup! Does that sound like something you'd rather do than listen to me? Huh? Because I can stop talking if that's what you want for your last moments of life."

With great effort, the injured man lifted his head, her signal to continue.

"I dislike having to be so rough with you, but it's for the best. I'm trying to entertain you and make you happy."

Leaning over she kissed him gently on the mouth.

"Where was I? Oh yeah, the game! So, of course it made me crave those beautiful, talking eyes. I wanted them so badly, but she wouldn't let me have them. It drove me crazy! Then my bus came. I was more sad than relieved, the torturous game was over, but without victory. I got on the bus happy to have played, even though it meant being away from her. It was the first time I had been happy about anything in a while, so I guess that's why I didn't notice her behind me as I walked down the aisle. As I turned to sit down, my heart skipped a beat. My lucky day! Before me the eyes I longed for told me to scoot over so she could sit down. I did as they requested, and she sat down right next to me. I couldn't help it. For what seemed like an hour, we just stared at each other. Then she said, 'Hi, my name is Eva.' That was the prettiest sound I had ever head a person speak. *Eva*. I said her name just to see if I could make the same beautiful sound. She smiled at me, then touched my hair and said, 'It's Eva as in forever.' It sounded even more beautiful when she put it like that.

"From that day forward, we were inseparable. She was just like me but without being a foster kid. Her parents had been stolen from her by drugs and prison. Her grandmother took care of her. She told me that once her mom got out of prison they would live together. Her dad was gone long before she could remember. Her grandmother called him junkie and as far as Eva knew, that was his nickname.

"I can't begin to tell you how in love I was with her. I couldn't wait to go to school. We would sit next to each other and pass notes in class. We would sit with each other at lunch and share our food. We would play together at recess, refusing to play with the other kids. We made it a point only to play games that would not attract our classmates. My favorite was when I would sit on a bench and she would stand on the opposite side of the playground. We would stare into each other's eyes until everyone on the playground disappeared. I really used to love that game.

"Her favorite game I didn't like very much, but I played it to make her happy. It was horrible! She would make me talk to other kids or grownups until she wanted me to stop. I hated it so much. The worst part was that these people would try to talk to me again only that time I wouldn't speak back. That was the other part of the game; they would speak to me and I would pretend not to even know they were there. Then they'd disappear and all I could see was Eva. Most of the time I'd only know other people were there when they touched me; as I've told you before, that's not something I like very much. So, I would scream. They would let go and then they would disappear for real, leaving only me and Eva. We played these games everywhere we'd go and slowly I began to reject everything but our world. I hated the real world; I was ten-years-old about to turn eleven. My foster home was a prison for children and love there was a bad word. I slept with a kitchen knife under my pillow and didn't have a reason why. I was just afraid.

"For my eleventh birthday, Eva and I planned to go stay at this castle where her uncle lived. She told me he was king of a country and he was going to give us our own city where we could be ourselves. Can you imagine having a whole city to yourself, with only your best friend to share it with? All we had to do was stay at his castle while they cleaned it and stocked it with our favorite foods. I couldn't wait to go. I couldn't wait to get away from everything but her and us.

"The day of my eleventh birthday, I went to school with a backpack full of clothes and waited at the hiding spot we'd picked to meet up. Hours passed but Eva never came. At some point, I went to sleep and awoke to darkness. The sky full of diamonds and Eva nowhere to be found. I didn't know what time it was. Afraid, I didn't move. Suddenly it came to me, I remembered that she was at the bus station waiting for me. Eva was going to be so mad at me for forgetting. I got up and began to run as fast as I could. The bus station wasn't too far away, maybe a couple miles. I ran and ran toward Eva and the bus station without exhaustion. I can't even imagine running that far today without stopping and I can't understand how I did it now, but I did. I made it to the bus station. That night it was so crowded. People everywhere; all grownups. I couldn't see over the towering adults. Then someone called my name. It sounded like her, so I ran in the direction of the voice. When I reached where I thought she was, all I found was a tall man standing, looking at me. He had eyes like Eva. He smiled and stuck out his hand greet me. I didn't move. 'Hi Cassandra. I'm pleased to meet you. My name is Shadow.' I didn't know him, but he knew my name. I refused to touch his hand. He knelt down so that we were face to face. I could see his wise and powerful features clearly. His presence entranced me.

"I woke up the next day on the bus alone, not knowing where I was. Shadow was gone, and Eva was still nowhere to be found.

"I looked around the bus and saw only strange faces. Unfamiliar people who didn't know me or where I was supposed to be. At eleven-years-old, I was free and in search of the castle where Eva should be."

Her victim vomited a green tinged foam and dry heaved, before vomiting again. The frothy remnants of the poison left as evidence in the corners of his mouth. She knew every gag must have been excruciating for him forced upright in his chair. She grabbed a wet towel and dabbed the corners of his mouth gagging at her victim's waste.

"Eva!" She screamed. "Help me clean him! This was your idea, it's disgusting!"

The man looked around his prison, but saw no one but his lone captor, whose voice shifted with her next words.

"This wasn't all my idea, Cassandra!" A voice rose from deep within her chest.

"Yes, it was your idea," her previous voice returned, "You said this would be the best way. You said talking to him would make me feel better. I want to stop!"

"No," bellowed the voice from deep within. "You talk to him until I tell you to stop. We are still playing the game. Now quit wasting time before he dies."

She slapped herself hard across the face.

"I'm sorry, Eva. I'm sorry. I'll play the game."

She stood up, straightened her clothes, and sat calmly in front of him again.

"As you can see, my search for Eva at her Uncle's castle was successful. The castle was as big as an entire city, but I found her. Yep... At her Uncle Sam's, and he could be real mean sometimes.

"We lived out in the hallways of his castle with other kids, working to get back inside the warm, furnished rooms. We'd all been banished and lived in fear of being caught by her Uncle's guards. If they found us they would throw us in the dungeon or make us go back to where we came from. I don't know if I wouldn't have been better off at a foster home. Life was hard in the hallways, but that was the price of freedom; whatever that is.

"You see this scar above my eye? Yeah, I got this my first night in the castle. We were in an old warehouse on her Uncle's property and I saw this older boy who was probably thirteen, sitting on a crate eating a sandwich. I couldn't remember when I ate last. Eva told me to ask him for a piece of it, so I figured it wouldn't be a problem. Cautiously I walked towards him, watching him eat his sandwich. He did not acknowledge me, but when I got within reach he looked up, then continued to eat as if I wasn't there. Hesitantly I spoke to him, 'Hello, my name is Cassandra, what's yours?' He acted as though he hadn't heard me, so I turned away. Then everything went black as the back of my skull erupted in pain. Crashing blows and explosive pain continued all over my head. I was being attacked! That boy eating the sandwich beat me until I was unconscious.

"When I awoke, I was on a bed in a makeshift tent constructed out of grey parachute with random boards holding it up. A candle nearby heated a can of food as well as the tent. The same boy that had beat me so savagely leaned over to open the can. I flinched in pain. I was scared Eva was gone."

An inappropriate laugh erupted from her full lips and hardened heart as she took sip of wine. She drew the liquid into her mouth slowly before returning to her somberness.

"The boy later told me his name was Gavin. Up until that point in my life Gavin was the only kid I had met that controlled his own destiny. He was my first teacher inside the hallways of the castle. That first day after he beat me unconscious his first words to me were, 'You're mine now. You belong to me. If you manage to get away I will kill you and anyone who's in my way of getting to you. Now eat!' I didn't say anything to him. Like the various boards holding up his tent, I was property. I belonged to him. He was only thirteen and everyone in the warehouse did what he said. Later in our relationship that made me feel good; being the property of the strongest.

"Still healing from the beating, he sent me out with some older kids the next day. I had no idea what to do. All he said was, 'Don't come back without food or money.' That's it! That's all. No direction, no nothing. Gavin's parting words to me were punctuated by my bruises, *just don't come back here without food or money.*

"We hit the trash strewn streets in search of treasure. The other kids broke off into groups, I just stood there trying to decide which way to go. A fat kid with a greasy face called out to me, 'Are you coming?' He was a foot taller than me and real ugly, but I was so happy to have direction, I just ran toward him and his bunch. I had no idea where we were going or what we were doing. I just didn't want to be alone.

"The kid who called my name was Zach. He was the pack leader of our roving group that day. It was me, him, and two skinny girls. I can't remember the other girl's names right now, but Zach sent me with a girl named Summer. She was really pretty, and her hair was green. We went behind a Chinese restaurant and dug through the trash. Summer showed me the value of moldy food. I must tell you, Charles, until you've looked for your next meal in a trash can, you haven't lived. Finding a half-eaten meal, sometimes a whole uneaten portion, was like winning a prize.

"We put what we found in zip-lock bags, then went to another dumpster at a Mexican restaurant, then a burger place, and we just repeated the process with each stop. When we were satisfied with our bounty we went back to the main hallway and begged for money from Uncle Sam's guests. Summer was smart. She used a hat and some dirt to cover up my beaten face. I caught a glimpse of myself in a clothing store window after my makeover. Dirt all over my face, but I didn't look beaten.

"At the end of the day in a back-alley Zach divided up the food and money in a process that seemed to have no methodology. Summer gave me a bag to put my food portions in and we went back to the warehouse. Gavin was watching me from the moment I walked in; his eyes locked on the bag in my hand. Trembling, I presented it to him. He ripped it from my palm without saying a word. The bag had a piece of pizza, some chicken chow-mein, pieces of steak and hamburger, and the money I'd bummed, probably about forty-five dollars. He seemed satisfied and he didn't hit me. I was relieved.

"That night we ate our garbage scraps, and everyone seemed to be smiling. Gavin sat next to me by the open fire and finally asked me my name. Our first conversation began while we watched the old furniture burn.

"As the light flickered in his brown eyes turning them gold he said, 'This world is not real.' I didn't understand. He said, 'Look around you. How many of us catch, kill, or harvest our own food? How many of us like the natural smell of man and woman? The smell of a man's breath without toothpaste? The reason he shaves his face, or she shaves her legs is because we are ashamed of who we are. It all reflects the fantasy.'"

The woman took a sip from her wine glass and studied the condition of her victim. The man could barely hold open his eyes. Death had entered the small space they shared. A deep voice rose once again from far within her and shot through the room, twisting her face in its production.

"I didn't tell you to stop, Cassandra!"

"I'm tired, Eva. You talk to him."

She gently set her wine glass down, as her face contorted again.

"Cassandra, you don't want to let me talk to him because I'm going to tell him the truth."

"I don't care, Eva! I just don't feel like talking to him anymore. Please let me stop! Please!"

"Fine, you big cry baby. You can stop for now. I want to talk to him anyway."

The woman before him smiled, her face still twisted, and rose from her seat. The man opened his eyes as best he could to watch her walk toward the lamp lying on its side where she stood it back upright. Her newly illuminated face was changed. Her eyes had grown even colder, her smile more devilish, even the tone of her skin seemed altered. Maybe he was just delirious from the poison.

"Hello, Charles," she purred, "my name is Eva. You've already met my dear friend, Cassandra. She really doesn't like to talk much but I, on the other hand, do. I love to talk. Especially to people that hurt us. *I* talked to Gavin, not Cassandra. She was afraid of him. She's always been like that, ever since the first day I met her.

"She was a quiet little thing that nobody paid attention to. It was like she was invisible or something. To tell you the truth, I didn't even know she was there until I caught her staring at me. So, I picked the kid up, put her under my wing, and we hit the road. She's not that bright, you know."

Eva leaned in so that she could whisper, "She really believes that shit about my Uncle Sam."

Her shrill laugh sent chills through the man's body.

"I went on the road in search of my father and she went on the road in search of freedom. Neither of us got what we wanted.

"My grandmother always told me to do what made me happy. I wonder sometimes if that had anything to do with us not being related. I wasn't her blood. My mom just dropped me off with her saying someday she would return. Well, I wasn't going to wait forever. So I grabbed Cassandra and left.

"I really don't know why she talks about this Shadow person. I've never seen him, but she always seems to. She's a little crazy, you know.

"Anyway, I don't know why I thought staying in a warehouse was a good idea. It was close to the bus station. Kids stayed there. I wasn't trying to get picked up by the cops, so it seemed a good idea. Well, that bastard Gavin took advantage of us. You know how we ended up leaving him? That asshole sold us. Typical man. Gets what he wants from you, then he's gone. He sold us to some low-life scumbag named Coke. A tall, thin, light-skin black dude, he was handsome with long wavy hair. Now *that* guy was some piece of work. He was a pimp. I was twelve-years-old."

Her eyes softened, widening as they filled with tears.

"Eva, I don't want to hear this. I don't want to think about Coke. Please stop, Eva. Please!"

As easily as they had softened, her eyes narrowed as they hardened with Eva's return.

"Shut up, Cassandra. I don't want to hear your whining. You said you wanted me to talk. Well, I'm talking. So you shut up."

The man noticed he couldn't fully feel his legs; paralysis had begun to consume him from the bottom up. Death crept slowly closer; though in his mind, it couldn't come fast enough.

"This bitch doesn't want to talk about it because she liked it. Every time I asked her to take care of him she did so without complaint. Now, I'm the bad girl. Fuck you, Cassandra!"

A thick silence blanketed the room. She pulled her hair back in a ponytail and regained her composure.

"Yeah, Coke was our second master in the house of Uncle Sam. The first night with him was memorable. He raped us in a cheap motel room and threatened to kill us if we ever left. How many times had we heard that one already?

"We were so young, he couldn't put us on the street. He kept us in motel rooms with his goons watching to make sure we didn't leave. Night after night, satisfying man after man, in hope of one day being satisfied ourselves. There was never a day off, and Cassandra was too afraid to do the work in the motels, so I had to do it. I had to do it every night. I always hated it, but when you do something enough you become numb to it. I became numb to the work, like every other job I have had. Just another day closer to death.

"One night, a customer spit in my face, slapped me and then urinated inside of me. Until you've felt that type of humiliation, you haven't been degraded. I almost wished he would have killed me, but he just wanted to degrade me even more. I don't remember much about that night. I just remember waking up on the floor looking at the puddle oozing from his head, the top of his skull smashed in with a hammer that Cassandra insisted we keep with us while I worked. Good thinking, huh?

"I had never seen a dead body before, so I walked up to it and stuck my fingers in the warm blood. It felt so good to see that bastard dead like that. If anyone deserved to be dead, it was him. I kicked him hard in the head and blood squirted everywhere. Parts of his skull cracked and spattered. Some of it got on my mouth. I didn't wipe it off, I licked it. It was the best thing I had tasted since entering the hallway."

She took her time, studying his beaten face as she moved closer to him. The man strained to watch her and flinched as she leaned in and licked his partially clotted, bloody face.

"You don't taste as good as he did," she laughed, "nothing is ever as good as the first time. Ever.

Well, Coke came to get us because I wouldn't open the door for anyone else. Cassandra insisted that we open the door for him. He came in all mad, but when he saw that body on the floor, he looked like he'd seen a ghost. That was the first time I'd ever seen fear in a man's eyes. His mouth fell wide open looking at the dead man on the floor and the sight of me covered in blood. At that moment, I knew I had power over him. We stood quietly, locked in place, staring eye to eye for what felt like an eternity until one of his goons came and recommended that we leave. We walked to the car in silence. The entire ride back to his house, a place I'd never been before that day, he did not say a word.

"The front of his home looked like a real castle complete with fountains, pillars, double doors, and a circular driveway filled with all different kinds of beautiful cars. We entered his house and two girls who didn't look that much older than me met us at the door in negligees; both were tall with hour-glass figures, one blonde, one brunette. He directed them to take me to the bathroom. They looked horrified by my bloodied appearance but did as they were told. We went into the bathroom where they undressed me and drew water for the bath. I must have looked like a zombie. They washed my hair and the rest of my body while I just sat there unable to wash my own body.

"The first time we spoke, Gina the brown-haired girl, was brushing my hair as the other girl, Lauren, watched. Gina asked me if I killed one of them. I looked in her eyes trying to see who she was, and I saw just as much pain as I felt. I introduced myself, 'Hi my name is Eva, on the street they call me Cassandra.' I guess that answered her question because she made no more mention of it and we started talking about our old lives, what we wanted to do in the future, how we liked to dress, and our favorite shampoo. Things like that were easy to talk about. We didn't talk about work; the sleazy service for money off the street.

"I woke up the next day to the smell of breakfast. I hadn't smelled home-cooked breakfast since I lived in foster care. Now, three years later, it still smelled the same. Since then I had begged for money on the street, dug through dumpsters for food, and lived in abandoned buildings for two years. I was fourteen years old and a professional prostitute. I had just woken up in a house the day after murdering a man, to the smell of breakfast being cooked."

She walked closer to her victim so that they were nose-to-nose, the smell of her breath intoxicating him even through the fog of her poison. Undeniably, she was a remarkable looking woman drunk off power and liquor. She spoke, "Do I look like someone who'd been through all that at fourteen? Oh Charles, nothing is ever what it seems."

She poured another glass of wine and ingested a pill, closing her eyes to savor the moment. The man watched her feeling the cold breath of death crawl up his body as she continued her story.

"Me, Gina, and Lauren became a team. We went on trips out of town. We served Coke's exclusive clientele and we ran his house. I had a lot of fun during those days. Cassandra and I barely talked.

"That's the funny thing about life, nothing ever stays the same. I can't stand it when things are going good for me because I know it won't last. At least when things are going bad, you can expect that they will eventually get better. It's never fun to go from happy to sad.

"Coke got busted. The Feds came and raided the house. I had a fake I.D., so I didn't get busted for being a minor. I figured it'd be better to go to jail as an adult than stay a minor and be sent back into the foster care system. I got busted for prostitution, kidnapping, and suspicion of accessory in a murder. I had never been finger-printed before, so I officially became an adult. I was seventeen-years-old.

"I had no idea why they gave me those charges. How did they know about me? How did they know what I had done? I could understand Coke getting busted, but why did they get me?

"That night I fell asleep in a cold cell after trying all night to figure it out. I had a dream while I was in jail that I found my father. It felt so real, not like I was dreaming. When I awoke the next day, I realized my father was the reason I went on this excursion in the first place. Then, for the first time I could remember I cried. I cried; and I cried for so long my tears led me back to an exhausted sleep.

"I awoke to a tall, burly, black man with a thick beard standing at the door. He was a sheriff. I sat up, immediately defensive. No man was worth anything good and I knew this one was here to bring me pain.

"He smiled at me, and said 'Now you're scared?' He dropped some papers on the floor, slamming the cell door closed. I could hear him laughing as he walked away down the hall; his laugh echoing into the distance.

"I was afraid. So, I went to the only safe happy place, back to sleep. A voice woke me. Cassandra. I was so happy to hear her. I knew she wouldn't ever leave me alone."

"No, Eva, I will never leave you alone. I will always be with you. I think I should tell this part of the story."

Tears ran down the woman's face. She was visibly shaken by something. Her eyes turned softer in Cassandra's tone.

"I read the papers to Eva. The words cut her like a knife. Her friend, Gina, had been working for the F.B.I. for at least two years wearing a wire. Eva didn't want to believe it. Besides me, Gina and Lauren had been her only friends ever. Finding out that friendship had been a lie hardened Eva from then on. She refuses to let anyone get close. There would be no more friends for me and Eva.

"I hated Gina. I wanted her to pay for what she had done, but honestly in that world what more could we expect?

"In the courtroom, I watched Gina recount all the things that Eva had shared with her in confidence. What kind of friend does that? What kind of friend tells your most personal thoughts to a room full of strangers? This is not a friend!

"Eva was found not guilty of the accessory to murder charge because the evidence was shaky. But she was found guilty of prostitution and kidnapping. The kidnapping was from an incident when Gina and Eva together lured a young lady into the life of prostitution. It was all Gina's idea. Eva received five years.

"Life in prison was no worse than living on the streets. We were still in Sam's house. Still living by Sam's rules.

"Time, we learned, was a thing of value. It's all we have in this world, and if we do nothing with it, it gives us nothing in return. That's the moment we began to spend our most valuable asset more wisely. Spending our moments knowing we will never gain them back. No more wasting time.

"Those five years flew by and soon we were back out in the streets. It was my duty to support us because Eva was too traumatized to enter the workplace. In prison, I became a skilled typist and learned computer software inside and out, then I got a job as a waitress. That's funny, huh? All of my qualifications and I couldn't even get a job in my field of expertise. No one would hire a convicted felon for office work so I waited tables on my feet all day. The customers were rude. The manager was disrespectful. The pay was horrible. After being a prostitute, the money I got for work like that was insulting. I was twenty-two-years old."

She paused for a moment and looked at the man. He was not unconscious yet, but he would be in a few moments and this was the part he needed to hear. Their reason for being here... Love.

"I knew she was an angel from the first time I laid eyes on her. I had never seen anyone more beautiful. I watched her eat her food. She'd take small bites until, like magic, the food was gone. I'd seen her in a dream before I met her. Seeing her in the flesh always seemed new, like it'd never happened before.

"One day at work, while my manager was yelling at me about something insignificant, I noticed her sitting in the same seat she had sat in the day before. My heart was pounding. I walked over, took her order, and watched her eat her food in her normal, delicate way. I wanted to say something when she looked my way, but I was frozen, and then she was gone. I was upset with myself for not talking to her more. What if... I could only hope that she would come back tomorrow.

"It was one of the longest days I can remember. Eight at night and the sun was still out. I decided to wash clothes at the laundromat. Loading the cool, wet clothes into the dryer was a joy. Taking them out was torture. It was hot. Turning to grab my soda I spotted her across the room. This time I wouldn't be a fool. I walked up to her, a walk that seemed to take forever. Our eyes locked as I moved toward her. When we stood face to face we said nothing. We just stared at each other. I felt as if I had known her all my life. 'Hi, my name is Rio.' She said."

Though barely alive, the man looked up upon hearing the name. The woman laughed knowingly at his recognition.

"That's why I lured you here. Did you think I was crazy? Did you think this was all some big mistake? You actually thought I was some innocent stranger that needed a lift home? You probably thought when I invited you up here that I would be another one of your conquests. Well Charles, you were wrong. You were really fucking wrong. This time you made a big mistake, the biggest mistake of your life."

She stopped pacing in front of the semi-conscious man and slapped him viciously across the face, sending a spray of bloody saliva across the floor.

"Rio lived here. The seat you're sitting in right now was her favorite. That day at the laundromat was the beginning of the happiest time I ever experienced. She was new in town and had been staying at a cheap motel while looking for a place to rent with a roommate. My face couldn't hide my flutter of excitement upon hearing she wanted a roommate. I jumped to offer her an invitation to stay here at this apartment with me.

"My feet didn't hurt anymore. I floated at work. A few days later while dumping the trash at the end of my shift, a deep and familiar voice vibrated into my body from behind. It was Shadow. When I least expected, he always came to show my reflection. He tried to warn me that Rio was a sign of death, one that I would see as love. By the time I turned around to see him, he was gone.

"I hadn't ever known love before. To be honest, I'd never really thought about it. I had come to believe that love was something I'd never know. But after that moment with Shadow, I began to wonder what it looked like, what it felt like. I started to think maybe I could have it too.

"That night when I came home she'd made me dinner. We ate

mostly in silence, keeping our mouths filled with food until all of it was gone. Words of acknowledgment and appreciation punctuated the silence. I felt like I didn't know her. Clearing the table, she began talking about where she came from as though she could read my mind.

"She'd grown up in a home with her mother and her stepfather, a minister. She hated her stepfather and from the look on her face when she said it I knew why. I sat on the couch. She put her head on my lap. I felt uncomfortably aroused. When she paused in her story I told her I had to go to bed. She stared at me knowing I was lying. I went in my room. That room right there, Charles. I went in that room and waited because I knew she was coming. I fell asleep and when I woke up during the night I was lying naked beside her. She was naked too with her arm around me and her head on my chest. No more sleep that night. I just stared at her until she woke up. The warmth between our eyes was all the *good morning* we needed. I asked her what her parents thought about her leaving. Stretching and yawning she told me the minister didn't care and her mother encouraged her to leave. That pulled me from bliss. Shadow's warning, a *sign of death disguised as love*.

"Eva and I weren't talking very much. She was hard to reach at times, still trying to piece her life back together. When we did talk it was only about her stuff. I knew she wouldn't want to hear this, so I had no one to confide in about Rio. Rio and I continued our dinners in silence. She watched me as I ate my food and I watched her as she ate hers until flashes of her naked body race through my mind. I wanted her so bad. I hadn't ever wanted a woman before. I fled. This time she smiled at my escape to the room. Knowing she was coming, I'd wait for her, but she only came after I fell asleep. The next morning, I lay naked beside her experiencing the various temperatures of our smooth bodies where they touched. Everything was finally completely perfect! I let my mind drift, lost in a comfort. Feelings I had never felt before were somehow still familiar. I realized I was smiling at her, thinking this can't be temporary, it felt too good, too real.

"Rio was so happy. She wanted me to pose so she could paint me. I had never done anything like that before, I went to the couch and posed. The way she moved her body while painting the canvas made it feel like the air around us was making love to every inch of my body. Her vision consumed me from every angle. I felt utterly naked as she peered into the depths of my heart. In the span of an afternoon, she'd finished her work. Before me was nothing I could have imagined. There I was, lying on a bed of snakes, one head though my face was blurry and divided, part happy and part sad. With the snakes around me, what looked like a lunar eclipse hung in the background, but I swear it was Shadow in the middle of clouds. Presiding over the whole image sat an angel resembling Rio arching her wings. I screamed, 'It's not me! It's not me!' until I woke up beside her, again naked.

"Do you see the painting Charles? Charles! Do you see the portrait? It's hanging on the wall! Charles, she painted this for me!"

The dead man's last breath had escaped moments ago. His body was still warm when she doled out her final vicious slap, sending the mucus which had hung thick from his nose across the room. His only response was the involuntary slumping of his body; fighting against the ropes still binding his wrists and ankles to the chair. The weight of his body won as the chair tipped and fell, his head landing with a heavy crack against the edge of the hearth.

She wished he wasn't dead. "Charles, you're making me angry. Stop joking. Now listen, while I finish telling this story."

"I walked into the sunlit kitchen singing when the horrid painting caught my eye from the living room. From the other room it taunted me with Rio's vision of me. I made her cover the painting. I could not bear to look at a picture that screamed my secrets and seemed to capture my whole life. I know the lunar eclipse is the face of Shadow. How could she know?

"The next evening after dinner, she stopped me as I tried to go to bed. Her hands gripped my shoulder. I felt chills on my arm as I tried to find my breath. 'Please sit down.' I didn't want to hear what she had to say. I was scared of what she knew. She stroked my hair gently as I nestled on the floor between her legs.

"She told me a story a story about a princess who had never known love. The princess lived in a magnificent castle in a beautiful kingdom. The only problem was that her father would not touch or talk to her, and he forbade her mother to see her for fear of a curse that had been placed on the family. If the King or Queen displayed any love to the princess she would die and if anyone else loved her, the royal family would lose their kingdom. So, at night the King would leave two guard dogs tied in front of her door so that no one could enter her chambers while the family was sleeping. Life for the princess was sad. No one would talk to her much less look at her. Her life was worse than a prisoner's.

"One night while she was sleeping, a beautiful, dark angel came to her window. It was the most beautiful thing that the princess had ever seen. The angel told the princess that she was here to watch over her, and she would always be safe as long as they were together; but the only way they could be together was if the princess trusted her enough to jump out of the tower window. The princess was afraid. The angel assured her that she would not be hurt if she jumped, but still the princess was unsure. The angel promised that she would love the princess and take care of her forever, but only if she trusted her enough to jump. The princess refused, and the angel disappeared.

"The next day the princess spent as usual, but the day seemed different. All she could think about was the angel, the beautiful angel with dark wings who promised to love her and take care of her forever. No one had ever promised to love her.

"That night in her chambers she waited, awake, all night but the angel never came. The princess woke next morning heartbroken. She hadn't ever felt this type of pain before. Again, another night she waited in her chambers for the angel and again the angel did not come. By the third night, the princess had given up all hope of seeing her again. As she started to fall asleep, she heard a voice whisper, 'Jump!' The princess was hopeful her angel had returned. Again, it said, 'Jump!' The princess rushed from the bed to the window hoping to see the angel, but the angel was not there. The princess stood at the window feeling the cool breeze of the night. She decided to step out onto the ledge. The stone wall was cold under her feet. She looked toward the ground knowing that if she was not caught, she would die. She jumped! She jumped off the ledge falling fast to the ground. In seconds, she would be no more, but she had never felt more alive. She closed her eyes as she headed to what she knew would be her doom. Then, she felt the softness of her angel's skin and they began to fly. She was in the arms of her angel who kept the promise to take care of and love the princess forever.

"When the King came to let his daughter out the next morning, to his surprise she was gone. He looked all over her chambers and found her nowhere. He leaned out of the tower window to alert the guards and to his horror he found his daughter lying dead. She had fallen to her death from the tower window. For the first time he wept for his daughter, and his tears remained relentless. Everywhere the King went, at some point he cried. His wife could not bear the loss of their daughter and she too jumped out of the same tower window. The beautiful kingdom was lost forever, but the princess had found love.

"That's a beautiful story isn't it, Charles?"

"I fell asleep as Rio brushed my hair. The soft smooth skin of her legs around me lulled me into a deep sleep. I went to a place that was absolutely beautiful. There, in this beautiful place, sat my angel atop a giant cloud. The cloud glowed with brilliant colors of red, yellow, and gold. Rio's wings were soft and fluffy. She opened them to embrace me. I was compelled by a force I cannot explain. I had no choice but to move in the direction of her embrace. I put my arms through her soft feathers expecting to push my arms through to the other side of her wings, but there was no end. My arms were stretched out inside her feathers as her wings began to move. The massive, fluffy wings closed around me covering us in darkness. At first, the darkness scared me but as I felt the warmth of her body next to me, the darkness became soothing. Her wings were like soft pillows caressing and massaging my back. I was in ecstasy. I floated there for a while in pure bliss. I tried to move but I couldn't. The embrace became tighter. I tried to move again, and it tightened even more. It seemed as if every breath I took made the embrace tighter. Suddenly I was having trouble breathing. I wanted to panic, but couldn't, for it would surely seal my fate. I began to wonder why, and she answered, 'I love you.' Her love was killing me.

"When I woke up she was standing over me smiling. The hideous picture I begged her to cover up loomed behind her. She stared deep into my eyes as if knowing that I had just dreamt about her. She laughed then said, 'Good Morning, Princess. Shadow has a message for you.'

"Charles. Charles," she said as though she expected him to answer. "When I first saw you, I knew that we would become close. Eva told me not to trust you, but I didn't listen to her. Even though you didn't notice me, I saw you."

She crawled over and kissed the dead man on the lips. The green foam from his regurgitation clung to her mouth in threads as she pulled away. She licked her lips and smiled.

"I'm sure you can imagine my surprise when I learned that she knew of Shadow. She claimed to know where to find him. I was eager to make that journey.

"We traveled on foot through the streets and into the forest. We left during the day, reaching the forest covered in darkness at night. Unfamiliar sounds echoed through the woods. The wind carries a more sinister sound in the forest after dark. I started to ask Rio how much further, but my words were replaced with crushing pain at the back of my head then everything went black.

"I woke up in a clearing of the forest, finally able to see the sky, again covered in diamonds. The great Shadow stood over me. Happy to see him I motioned to get up but was quickly restrained and blindfolded by two women I had never seen before. The great Shadow spoke, 'For years I climbed this mountain of obstacles and pain not knowing what my reward would be for reaching the top. Many days I thought about giving up. Some days I thought I would not make it. One day I reached my destination; the top of the mountain. Finally, at the top I searched for my reward, but all I found was me. My journey allowed me to find myself. This journey, all must take. Reach inside yourself and answer the question of what you are here for!'

"Hands began to disrobe me; so many more than just Shadow and the two women. Shadow then said to me, 'If you know the touch of your love, call out to her when you feel her caress. If love is not touching you and you call out, love will disappear forever!' The multitude of hands massaged my body from head to toe, so many hands touching, I couldn't figure out which ones were hers. I began to cry because I knew that if I guessed wrong she would be gone forever. I called out to her as a plea. I screamed her name thinking it would be the last time she'd hear me, and the hands stopped. All the hands disappeared except for one over my heart and one over my head. The blindfold was removed. Rio's eyes were the first thing I saw. We made love in front of the great Shadow. I had found what I was here for - her.

"We spent the next few weeks with only each other. Every moment seemed to bring us closer. Every second seemed to be filled with something to treasure. Then the landlord came around for the rent money and we didn't have it. One day I had just stopped going to work at the diner. I don't even remember when. I told Rio that I could get the money. She knew about my past. She knew I knew how to survive and she refused to let me do it. She went out the next day early in the morning looking for a job. I sat at home waiting for her, angry that the time she would spend working was time we couldn't be together."

"I want to tell this part of the story, Cassandra." Eva interrupted.

"Eva, I don't want to stop talking now."

"I said shut up, Cassandra! We are still playing the game. It's your turn to be quiet." She crawled over to the dead man and shook her head. "You dumb ass bitch. He's dead! You've been telling the story to a dead man. He will never get to hear the best part of how I saved the day and came up with this plan. If it wasn't for me, you'd still be walking around like a lovesick puppy."

"That's not true, Eva! Rio and I were fine until you came back. You came back and ruined everything."

"You ungrateful little bitch! I've taken care of you since you were a little girl, and this is the thanks I get? You tell me that this is all my fault? I saved you! What happened when Rio came home that day? What happened?"

"Eva, stop!"

"Stop? Why? You're so eager to keep talking. Now you can. Since you seem to think this is my fault, tell me what happened when she came home!"

"I – I hate you, Eva. I can't wait until this is over." Sobbed Cassandra.

"Neither can I! Go ahead, finish the story!"

With a deep breath, Cassandra stood up and began the end of their story.

"Rio came home happy that day. She rushed through that door with energy I had never seen before. She hugged me tight, kissed me, and said she'd found a job. I was happy that she was happy, but I couldn't hide my selfish disappointment. Rio asked me what was wrong. I told her I didn't look forward to spending time apart and I couldn't understand how she could be so happy about it.

"My tears brought her tears and we both contributed to the salty puddles before us. She apologized for thinking only of the rent, and not the time it forced us apart. I knew how important it was for her to take care of us. Each feeling selfish for not seeing through the other's eyes, we ate dinner, and then went to sleep.

"That night I had a dream Rio and I were being held apart by a wall. I could hear her calling me and I desperately wanted to get to her. I tried to climb the wall, but it only got bigger as I moved. I chiseled at the wall but the holes I created filled up once I got close to the other side. I called out to her as I pounded the stone with all my strength. On my first strike I cracked it, and just like that the wall came crashing down. As the dust settled I called out to Rio but I heard nothing. I called to her again, still nothing. Finally, the dust cleared, and I could see. On the other side of the wall was a church filled with people looking at me. At the pulpit stood a boy in a football uniform and Rio in a beautiful wedding dress. She turned around and said she never loved me. Vengefully I grabbed at her, catching her veil, I pulled her back toward me. Her neck split in half and I was covered in her blood. I dropped to my knees screaming and that's how I woke up, screaming all alone in the bed. Rio had already left for her first day at work."

"Is that what you wanted to hear, Eva?"

"No Cassandra, that's not what *I* wanted to hear. I wanted *you* to hear it 'cause you seem to be blaming me for what happened, yet I don't hear my name in any of this story. *I* remember keeping you company while you waited for her to come home. *I* remember helping you plan, prepare, and cook dinner for her. I also remember having to hide because you didn't want her to know I was there. Do you want to know a secret? *She knew I was there.* The nights you can't remember are the nights that I do. You have no idea what kind of passion Rio & I shared on those nights you don't remember when you woke up naked the next morning. I got chills every time she touched me. We made love every time you blacked out and had those ridiculous dreams. You always upset me with those stupid dreams.

"I want you to remember something. What happened after a few weeks of Rio working? Who told you to go down to her job and see how she's doing? Who?"

"That's what I mean, Eva! I should have never gone down there! I should have never gone to see her there!"

"Why not, Cassandra? Why shouldn't you have gone down there? Why?"

"Because Eva! Because ..."

The woman dropped to her knees, vomiting until she was weak and drained. She lay on the floor unable to move herself out of the pool of her own vomit. The pill she'd taken earlier had begun to take hold of her spirit. Mumbling, she continued where she'd left off.

"Because I saw him... I saw Charles. I knew when I saw him that he was the reason why she was coming home late, the reason why she wouldn't touch me anymore. I listened to you Eva, I went there many nights and watched them, heartbroken. I listened to you and I said nothing to her about what I saw, or what I felt. I just lay there at night hoping she would touch me, and she never did."

The woman dry-heaved in anguish until she produced a thick clot of mucus wrapped in blood.

"When I told Rio about my dream with the wall she was silent. Then she cried. She told me that's why she left. She'd left to get away from the pain of not being able to with her first love."

A tear rolled down the woman's face, into her puddle of vomit. Her body convulsed and spasmed as it tried in vain to rid itself of the poison.

"I wasn't her first love. I – I did not know my own love. The thought of someone else having my love instead of me... And you, Eva, you filled my mind with horrible thoughts. You – you told me that it was all Charles' fault and that we had to do away with him. You told me that if he died, then I would possess love. Well, he's dead and I still don't have her!"

"You stupid little bitch! You poisoned me! You're going to kill us, Cassandra? Why... Why? We made him pay. Rio will love us again. We still haven't found what we're looking for. We are still playing the game."

"Eva, the game is over. We have both lost and I don't want to play anymore."

Her fearful whimpers were faint beneath her short, labored breaths.

"I – I don't want to die, Cassandra. Please, don't... Please don't do this."

"I'm not doing anything Eva. We did this! We found out why we were here and now it's time for us sleep and dream... It's the only way out of this castle, Eva."

"I don't want to go, Cassandra. I don't want to."

"Shhhh, Eva. I came here with you. Now it's time that you come with me. It's time to leave here."

The woman closed her eyes and silence overtook the room.

The door to the apartment opened. The woman on the floor opened her eyes and saw a beautiful angel. The angel floated over to the woman and lifted her head from the vomit, tenderly cradling her head in her soft, dark wings. Through troubled breaths, the woman's final words left her lips.

"Please forgive me beautiful angel. You told me if I leapt from the tower window that you would catch me and take care of me forever... I – I knew you would catch me... I knew you would. Now I will be with you always. That's what I was here for... To be with you." The woman smiled looking off into the distance, "...there goes Shadow."

The angel kissed her gently on the forehead as she said her own goodbye.

"My beloved sister Eva, I wish I could have told you that we were family, but I was forbidden to do so. You didn't even know that you had succeeded in your quest of discovering who you are. You found your father and a sister that you didn't even know you had. Charles was our father, Eva! Mama named you that. 'Cassandra' is who you were meant to be. This world created Eva, and you created Cassandra. I love you, sister."

She kissed the woman again then grabbed a nearby pillow and placed it underneath her head. At the door she stood for a moment looking at the remains of her family, her father and sister both dead on the floor, remembering times she shared with each. Then she turned and went back into the hallways in the house of Sam.

Part Two
The Family Friend

Ethan lay in bed looking out at the oak tree he had climbed as a kid. It was the first day of his senior year in high school, his last moments as a boy in the adult world; he would now take his place among men. Smoothly reaching out to the night stand he grabbed his phone, turned off the unnecessary alarm and sat up in bed. Catching a glimpse of himself in the mirror Ethan could not help but admire the honey complexion staring back for a moment. His dark hair was perfectly cut, ready for his debut. He knew he was easy on the eyes and found it hard to resist his own baby blues when he caught his reflection. Breaking away from the mirror, he got up.

The phone summoned his attention again. Barry was calling.

"B, what's up man? What's going on?"

"Coach said we have mandatory practice today after school. Are you prepared, Smith?" Barry said, changing his voice to mimic their coach. "Are you prepared to meet the challenges that face you on the field? It's not a football field, it's a battlefield and we are at war! Can you look your enemy in the eye and show no fear? Huh, Smith? Can you do that?"

Ethan smiled at Barry's impression of their coach.

"Man, you're nuts, B! I'll see you at school, dude."

"E, Hold up. Can you come pick me up? Pulling up with my mom is lame. First impressions are everything and those freshman chicks have got to see me for who I am. Best friends with the star quarterback! You can't have your wingman pulling up with his mom in a station wagon first day senior year."

"You better be ready when I get there or you're walking to school."

"I stay ready, E. Later man!"

An hour later Ethan slowed his white Mustang to a stop in front of Barry's house. With the top down Ethan looked like a movie star.

Already outside, Barry jumped in without opening the door and the two were off to their first day of senior year in high school. Their drive didn't involve much talking. The stereo system's pounding bass announced their arrival as they both made sure to look as cool as possible. Other commuters stared at the fine piece of machinery while the two boys acted as if they didn't notice. When they reached campus, all eyes turned to them. It wasn't just the car, it was Ethan Smith, star quarterback who had never lost a game and had never been denied a date with any girl in school. Once parked, a small crowd began to form around the car; a natural occurrence for the star.

"Mr. Smith!" A voice yelled from behind the gathering. Ethan, annoyed that someone had interrupted his grand entrance, scanned the crowd for the familiar voice. Dominic, a small boy with an oversized backpack and ill-fitting clothes was parting the grove of onlookers and making his way toward the car. Ethan had found various uses for him throughout the years. "Mr. Smith, I have your class schedule here. If you want me to make some changes let me know by the end of the day and I'll hook you up."

Ethan reviewed the paper nodding his head with approval. "Thanks Dom! I'll check these classes out and let you know by the end of the day if I like them. Matter of fact, stop by my table at lunch. I'll have something for you."

The young genius lit up with excitement, hurrying to disappear back into the crowd. "Thanks Mr. Smith! I'll see you at lunch time."

As Ethan emerged from the white horse with Barry, his thoughts were on his audience; plenty of new faces to be seduced and many old faces that needed attention. A king and his castle. The last year of his reign; he'd have to make it memorable. They deserved at least that much from him for all their dedication.

Ethan walked to his first class with a parade of courtiers behind him. They stopped as he stopped, following where he went. These courtiers were not random fans, but the top kids in school. Those he'd either given power to or had recognized as valuable to his power, whom he'd allowed into his entourage. Ethan knew that by having powerful people at his side, he became even more powerful.

As the parade made its way through the hallways he could almost hear the envy of the students looking on. One by one he dropped the courtiers off at their classes saying hello to their teachers as if he were part of the faculty. No one would lead this crowd but him! None would taste his position. Subjects could become envious, but courtiers could not. At the slightest hint of jealously against their king he would ignite the group to settle it utilizing mob mentality. He fostered their dislikes and differences amongst each other creating silent treaties under his direction. By doing this he'd never actually be seen doing the dirty work himself. He would simply take his blessings away and allow others to shun the offending party. In this manner, Ethan crystalized his image as pure among his followers, giving himself room to maneuver at leisure.

His first class, math, he arrived at with the last of his courtiers. Barry dropped him off with a handshake and a one-armed hug. The teacher was not there. Ethan scanned the room for one of his aides knowing Dominic had taken care of everything. Noticing contempt in the eyes of an old girlfriend, he smiled and continued searching. Found. His target, the person who would do all his work for this class, a kid busy writing notes for a class that had not yet begun.

"Ian!" He called out, walking toward the young man. "Ian! What's up dude? I didn't see you at the pre-season game last week. What's up with that, man? You're supposed to be our biggest fan! We almost lost the game because you weren't there."

The chubby, freckled faced young man looked up at Ethan and grinned, pushing up his glasses.

"Um, I'm sorry Quarterback Smith, but I had a science fair I had to attend. I won first place."

"That's cool Ian! Are you going to have to miss any more games? Because you know we need you, man."

"No way Quarterback Smith! I won't miss another game this

season. I designed new routes for you guys to consider."

"Aw, that's killer Ian! I can't wait to check them out."

"Yeah, I'll have them at practice this afternoon."

"Cool. Cool. I'll see you there, Ian."

Ethan walked off to a seat already reserved for him in the back-right corner of the class. This was his seat in every class and everyone who attended the school observed this unspoken rule. Deny the star quarterback anything and you'd turn the entire school against you. The teacher had arrived and began the lesson, as if on cue Ethan put his headphones on and began playing on his phone. The day would continue like this until gym, which went right into football practice. At lunchtime, his group converged at the designated meeting area, so they could walk to their tables in entourage. They embodied the essence of cool as they strolled in a pack, laughing and talking as if life were that simple.

Seated at their table, macho stories and laughter in unison at similar punchlines attracted flirtatious looks from new girls. Ethan couldn't care less about the attention; he barely glanced around the cafeteria. He had worked hard for this recognition, but now that he'd achieved it he couldn't help wondering what was better than this? What else could excite the passion on which he'd built his kingdom?

Drained by the day's performance and with waning enthusiasm for his kingdom he entered his final class before gym, social studies. Immediately Ethan was thrown off balance by a disruption in his manicured kingdom. His initial surprise turned quickly to annoyance as an incredulous crowd looked on. In the back-right corner of the room, someone was sitting in his seat. The girl seemed oblivious to the violation. The consummate charmer, Ethan disguised his annoyance with a friendly smile.

"Excuse me, Miss, you're sitting in my seat."

The girl looked up at him, rolled her eyes, and looked back down. In that brief moment, Ethan felt something he hadn't felt in a long time: a challenge.

"I didn't see your name on it when I sat down." She said in a snappy, matter of fact tone.

Stunned by her defiant reply, Ethan kept his composure masking her slight against him with his award-winning smile.

"That's because you weren't looking hard enough," he said with a chuckle. "Do you mind?" He moved her books aside to expose his name carved in the desk.

"You can see my name more clearly now without these books in the way."

Students within earshot began to laugh.

"I'm Ethan Smith, star quarterback of the Skyline Spartans. That name on the desk will one day be in lights. So tomorrow bring your phone and take a picture so you can tell your kids that you met me."

The other students' laughter rose. The girl sighed heavily, grabbing her belongings. Ethan maintained his smile. The girl looked him up and down, looked at the desk and said, "Take a picture of you? You're just another guy that can play ball. There were guys before you and there will be guys long after you are gone. So here is your seat. Enjoy it!"

She rose, returning his coquettish grin in mockery. No girl had ever given him such a brazen attitude. He watched her glide to another seat as if she was the winner of the territory battle. *Who was she?* Was her sitting in his seat an attempt to catch his attention? If that was her plan, it worked. She had his full attention.

"That will be your first homework assignment for this course, so please complete and turn it in tomorrow at the start of class." The teacher's voice startled Ethan back into reality.

Students moving past him to leave the class didn't deter his interest in the subject at hand. He positioned himself to perfectly block her path, his charming facade in full effect.

"Excuse me, Miss, but you never told me your name."

She looked with a smirk. "You're right I didn't tell you my name. Excuse me, I've got another class to attend." Stepping aside to let her pass he smiled to hide his disbelief. She slid past him, laughing.

At practice Ethan regained the confidence he felt when he first arrived at school. No girl had ever spoken to him in such a dismissive manner. This was *his* school and she was merely a student in attendance. She *must* understand her place, but first he needed to know more about her. With his confidence in its full glory after a show stopping practice, Ethan was eager to begin his most challenging subject. He sat in his car and laughed to himself, marveling at how easy it is to learn. It took less than a ring before the other end answered. "Dom, I need a favor."

The next morning Ethan rose with vitality and thirst for the day. Dominic had given him all the information the school's records could provide on the mystery girl. A few puzzling questions remained: first, as she had been home-schooled all her life, why enroll in public school for her final year? Next, her address was far outside the district. So far in fact, it made absolutely no sense why she would travel all that way to go to Skyline when a better school was much closer to her house. Dominic said no family members or anyone from the faculty had recommended her, so why had she chosen Skyline? These questions raced through his head as he drove to pick Barry up for school. Barry hopped in the car and knew in an instant. He looked at Ethan with the kind of concern Ethan would only accept from him. Ethan returned his look with one of annoyance, *what are you looking at?* He thought. Barry smiled.

"E!" He said with a giggle. "Who is it this time?"

Ethan was unamused. "What the hell are you talking about?"

Barry knew he was on shaky ground, so he approached with caution.

"Hey, man," he said in a softer tone. "You looked like something was on your mind. Usually that means somebody pissed you off. Did Coach say something to you about practice yesterday?"

Cracks in the shaky ground opened up. How dare Barry think his abilities on the field at practice could be questioned. Ethan pulled the car to a stop.

"What makes you think that Coach would ever come down on me? Huh? When I play my worst, it's ten times better than anyone else on the team. If you have a problem with the way I'm looking this morning you can get out of my car and find another way to school."

Barry froze. He had had it too good with Ethan in his life. He'd gone from the fat kid in elementary to the second most popular guy in high school because he was Ethan's best friend.

"Are you gonna speak or get the fuck out of my car?"

Barry swallowed, quivering under Ethan's threat. "I didn't mean anything by it, E. You're my buddy, man, I noticed at practice yesterday, you played well, but you just weren't yourself. Then you pulled up this morning not playing any music, with the top up, staring straight ahead. You didn't even look over when I got in the car. My bad, bro."

Ethan's expression of anger remained unchanged. "Sometimes I do shit different, B, and I don't want you or anyone else questioning me when I do that."

Barry breathed a sigh of relief to still be in the car. "Yeah E, I understand."

Ethan turned the music on and put the top down.

At school Ethan resumed the normal routine, acting his usual self, but with a great change in his thoughts. A king without sport doesn't last long. He knew every class that his new prey would attend. His spies watched her to learn her habits and patterns. A skilled hunter, he would not rest until he finally captured the trophy.

There was no observable difference from yesterday to today; the mask Ethan wore showed nothing but the observer's reflection. He passed her by as if he hadn't noticed, yet every move he made was calculated. He wanted her to see him, to know him, but he controlled her growing knowledge, and he knew just how to pique her interest. It would all be on his terms; she'd never know how meticulously he curated her curiosity. He savored each moment their paths crossed with the thrill of an assassin watching the mark, knowing that soon he would strike. For the star quarterback, this was more exciting than a spirit rally before game time. He was prepared to wait days, weeks, or even months for the perfect strike.   A few weeks went by and Ethan was sitting in social studies class still pretending to ignore his prey. Potential suitors had come her way, but she had refused them. He wondered why she'd turned them down. They weren't bad looking. Spies reported she stayed mostly to herself. Ethan found that news strange; most people fit in somewhere. He figured outside of school had to be it for her. A few days passed by, and opportunity arose. One of Ethan's spies found her studying at a coffee shop close to her house and had also seen her painting after school at a nearby rose garden. He'd found a key to unlock the door. He would need his best worker to infiltrate her world and bring her closer to him before he could strike.

"Denise!" Ethan's voice boomed through the hallway. "Denise!" The crowded hallway lowered the noise, so their king's words could be heard. A beautiful girl paused her conversation, turning with a sweet look to acknowledge him. The hush that had overtaken the halls hummed back to its previous volume and everyone returned to what they had been doing. Ethan approached the girl whose flowing chestnut hair carried the fragrance of rose, eyes that glowed like a sunset, and amber skin as smooth as marble.

"Hey Ethan, what's up?"

"Niecey, I need a favor from you. Walk with me for a minute."

As he walked toward her students in the hall moved to accommodate his entourage, while the two walked out of ear shot.

"I need you to befriend someone for me."

"Yeah, E, you know I'll do whatever for you. Let me know what's up."

"Okay, look, there's this new girl at school and I want to know where she's from. You know the game we play?"

"Yeah E, I know. What do you want me to do?"

"She goes to a coffee shop across town to study after school and sometimes she draws at the rose garden. I want you to go to those places, make friends, and bring her back to me."

"Yeah, E, I got it. Give me all the information and I'll go there after school."

"Perfect, Niecey, I'll call you in a few days. While we're at school I want you to act as if you don't know me, okay?"

"Okay. We'll talk in a few days, E."

After practice that evening Ethan arrived home to find his dad waiting for him. His job took him away on business a lot. He'd rarely be at home for longer than a month before taking off again on another trip. Ethan longed for the days when his father was home more, and they could spend time talking together, playing catch, or going for pizza after practice. Ethan admired him and owed the creation of his kingdom to the wisdom passed down from his father.

In his deep, authoritative tone, his father beckoned, "Sit down and talk to me about how things are going with you. It's been a while since we talked man to man."

Ethan assessed his seating options and chose the couch instead of the recliner. His father, smiling with approval remained standing.

"Son, you have always been smart when it comes to handling affairs in your life. I commend you on that. It's not always easy being a young man. A lot of pressures come from your peers that may tempt you in the wrong direction. I came here for you, son; I'd like to know how you're doing."

Ethan approached the question with caution.

"Well, Dad, I'm doing as well as can be expected, getting ready for college. I'm preparing myself for that transition, and I'm pretty much just maintaining my normal routine with training and practicing for football."

The older man grinned, as if each of his son's words meant the world to him. His smile faded into sorrow as he let out a deep sigh. This strong, powerful man seemed on the verge of tears. What could cause a man's countenance to change so quickly?

"Pop, are you ok?"

His father's arms shot straight out swift and stiff, signaling Ethan to stay away. "Ethan, I don't know how to tell you this, but your mother and I are getting a divorce. Things have been different between us for quite some time. We thought things might work out, but it's better if we're apart. I love your mother a lot, but we have grown in different ways over the years…"

After the word 'divorce,' his father's voice faded until no sound came from his moving lips. Ethan was old enough to deal with the situation, but not old enough to accept the fact: A divorce!

That night Ethan's thoughts were filled with too much pain to accept the tranquility of sleep. His father stayed at a hotel while his mother cried herself to sleep. Desperately wanting to cry, Ethan would not allow tears to come. Ethan evaded sleep until the sun's rays pierced the lingering tendrils of the night, it was then when he vowed not allow his parents' divorce. With this vow, Ethan finally found an hour's rest before school.

"Mr. Smith!" Dominic shouted as he ran down the hall toward the cruising entourage. "Mr. Smith!" He yelled. "I have something important to tell you." The crowd stopped and allowed the young man through.

Ethan turned around smiling, politely excusing himself from a conversation with two girls, who giggled at the nerdy-looking Dominic.

"What's up, Dom?"

"I'm sorry to bother you like this, but Ms. Howard wanted me to tell you that she has made contact and will speak with you tonight."

Grinning at his success Ethan put his arm around the messenger's neck, flexing his muscle to apply the precise amount of pressure to the hold. With his mouth close to the young man's ear, Ethan whispered.

"Stop yelling my name when you need to speak with me. All you need to do is walk up and request a moment of my time. Do you understand?"

The pressure around the messenger's neck grew more intense. "Yes, Mr. Smith. I will not call your name out loud like that again. I'm -- I'm sorry."

Ethan released his hold and fixed the young man's shirt collar.

"I'm glad we could work that out, Dom! You tell Denise I'll meet her tonight at 8:00, over at the lake."

"Alright, Sir. I'll tell her." The young man scurried off through the crowd and Ethan resumed his conversation.

Ethan reached the meeting point an hour early so that he could watch who came and went. The lake was a secluded area covered in a canopy of trees, amid a landscape sprinkled with meadows. A place for family bar-b-ques by day and a rendezvous point for young couples at night. Most weekends you could find teenagers gathered around a keg or two, but tonight the place was deserted. Ethan climbed a tree by the front entrance, gaining a panoramic view of the entire scene. As he sat in his perch, he thought about his parents and how he was going to be a hero by bringing them back together. He could see by their reactions that they must still love each other. He couldn't imagine all of them being alone in the world; him at college, his mother at home and his father God knows where. That thought troubled him greatly. He knew there was a way. He just had to figure it out.

At 7:59 Denise came through the entrance. He watched her walk timidly beneath the trees, her arms folded across her chest. Despite her buttoned coat, he could see her beautiful figure in the darkness. As she passed under the tree he jumped down landing behind her, eliciting a scream that shattered the calm of dusk.

"Calm down girl, damn!" He said, rubbing his left ear. "You knew I would be here."

Her hand was over her heart as she worked to catch her breath.

"You scared me! I wasn't expecting you to jump out of a tree."

"You're right, my bad." He said wrapping his arms around her. "Everything is gonna be alright. I got you girl. You don't have to worry about anything now."

She grew calm with his arms around her, feeling the warmth of his body. Her fears drifted away in his embrace, she never felt safer than in his arms. Ethan pulled back just enough to look in her eyes. Her breath caught in her throat and her heart seemed to stop. She blinked, and all thoughts vanished from her mind. At that moment, all that existed was him.

"Niecey, you alright honey?"

The words brought their surroundings into focus and she felt the earth beneath her feet again.

"Oh yeah, I'm cool. I'm cool."

His fingers slid down the back of her arm, taking her hand in his. "You want to walk over to the water?"

"Yeah. I'd like that."

The two walked casually, speaking of the fun times they had shared at the lake, laughing as they reached a bench in front of the water. The moon cast a shimmering reflection on the lake's glassy surface. The whole park seemed to glow in silver moonlight. With his arm around her, Ethan pointed to the moon.

"I've never seen it shine so bright, Niecey. Maybe it's because I'm with you, huh?"

She smiled back, "No, Ethan, it's because *I'm* with *you*."

He nodded, bringing a more serious tone to the conversation. "I guess it's good that we're together."

"Yeah, I guess it is."

The two sat in silence a moment, then Ethan spoke. "So, what's up with our new stranger?"

Near midnight Ethan came through the door of his house. The place held a new kind of quiet and darkness. He had lived there all his life, yet he now felt he was entering a strange new world. Before reaching his room, Ethan peeked in on his mother. Her room glowed with light from the television, left on while she slept, snoring lightly. An empty bottle of vodka surrounded by crumpled tissue paper told the story of her night. Ethan's heart ached seeing her in so much anguish. Covering her with a blanket, he gave her a kiss on the cheek and turned off the television.

Reaching his bedroom all he wanted to do was sleep, but he had to remove the smell of Denise from his body. Sleeping with the smell of a woman's body on his skin was something he would never do. In the hot shower he let the water wash away all his worries for a moment, reflecting only on Denise's account of the new, mysterious stranger in his kingdom. The new girl, Rio, was attending Skyline because it's the best high school for the arts.

The week flew by for Ethan and it was finally his night to shine for all to see. The first home game of the regular season and the stands were packed with fans, all wearing the school's colors. Ethan took to the field and the crowd erupted in pent up excitement. The kingdom was happy to receive their king. Ethan scanned the crowd for his father's face; he'd promised to be at the opening game.

"Smith!" Coach yelled from the sideline, "Smith!" Coach yelled again. "Get your ass over here!"

Ethan hurried over to where the coach was standing.

"Aye, coach, what's up?"

"Your father called. Said he's going to be late. He wanted to let you know before the kick off."

Ethan nodded, "Thanks, Coach!"

"You're welcome kid! Now get your ass in there and win this

damn game."

Ethan was a bit on edge as he played through the game. His father always had that effect on him. He played the game to his best ability, but it wasn't until the third quarter when his father appeared on the sideline next to the coach that the game became a blur of connections and touchdowns. By the time the referee called the game, Ethan had four touchdown passes and had rushed for a touchdown himself. They had blown the other team out of the water but having his dad on the sideline gave Ethan a feeling better than any game he'd ever won.

"Dad!" Ethan ran from the crowd on the field to the sideline, his helmet in his hand, "Dad! How'd you like the game? Scouts think I'll make pro!"

His father was beaming as he looked at the glow of child-like excitement in his son's eyes.

"Go pro?" He said. "Go pro? You're going to be the greatest quarterback that ever lived! People will tell their grandkids about games they saw you play in. You're a living legend son!" His arm stretched around his boy's shoulder. "Now you go get cleaned up, so we can grab something to eat."

"Alright, Pop."

Shaking more hands and accepting accolades, Ethan made his way into the locker room. His teammates were headed to a party at Barry's house. Ethan really wanted to go join his teammates, but as his father had always told him, *A true king must always sacrifice what he wants, to have what is best."*

Ethan was going for the best thing he could imagine, and that was his parents getting back together. He exited the locker room and was greeted with a surprise that made his heart skip: Denise and Rio coming his way.

"You played a great game!" Rio said.

"Yeah," Denise purred, "you played a great game."

Ethan maintained his cool, even though his heart was beating rapidly.

"Thanks, ladies! I really appreciate that. I'm sorry if I'm being rude, but there's somewhere I need to be right now, so you'll have to excuse me."

Rio looked at him playfully. "Are you on your way to Barry's party? Because that's we're going!"

It was just what he had been waiting for, the opportunity to strike his target.

"I don't know. I'll try to make it later, but right now I have to go. Excuse me ladies." He left the two young women in wonder as he rushed to the car where his father was waiting.

The ice cream parlor was the place for families after a winning game, and tonight was no exception. Ethan and his dad didn't wait long for a table, there always seemed to be room for the star quarterback. Ethan remembered going there as a kid and watching the team's quarterback courting the town's attention like royalty, thinking one day that would be him. Ethan's father would tell him, *"Every position must be fulfilled by an able body, and a true leader will rise by knowing how to play every position."* Now Ethan was the star quarterback looking into the eyes of young boys who wanted someday to fill his position.

"Great game, Ethan!" Mrs. Robinson said, her three small children gathering around her.

"Yeah champ great game!" Mr. Davis said, patting Ethan on the back.

A young boy held out his football. "Will you sign my ball?"

This was Ethan's reward for his many years of hard work and all the days he had to sacrifice the fun things he wanted to do so that he could reach the goals he sought.

"Okay, okay, that's enough, people!" Mr. Johnson, the portly owner of the ice cream parlor, announced as he put his arm around Ethan. "I'm sure our star quarterback would like to enjoy his favorite sundae with his father."

Ethan handed the signed ball back to the young boy. "Someday this team will be yours if you work hard. Stay focused kid!"

Sitting with his father, Ethan searched for the proper thing to say, but the energy of the moment didn't fit his feelings.

"I'm sorry I was late to your game son, but I had some important business to take care of that came up unexpectedly."

Ethan wanted to lash out about the business that was destroying his family, but he held his tongue. "Dad, why are you and Mom getting a divorce when it seems like you both still love each other so much?"

His father closed his eyes, as if searching for right words to say. "Son, I love your mother very much and I know this divorce is tearing us both apart inside, but we just can't be together anymore. When you get older you will understand. It's very complicated."

Ethan stared at his father wondering why he had gotten such an ambiguous answer. Instead of pushing for more, he would do what great kings must do, discover the answers for himself. "Dad, can you and mom attend my next home game together, for me?"

His father looked down solemnly at his ice cream, then back up at his son. "I will be there, Ethan, but it's up to your mother if she would like to attend."

"Alright! I really appreciate that. I'll talk to Mom about it."

Having them back together, if only for one moment of happiness, would be a step closer to his plan.

Barry's street was lined with cars. Music blared into the neighborhood and kids were walking to and from the house. On the front porch and lawn kids were making noise, laughing and talking. Through the window Ethan could see people dancing. This was typical after a game.

"E-Nut!" Barry screamed, alerting the others their champion had arrived.

"Man, this party is off the chain, dude. Go Spartans! Go Spartans!

Go! We are some muthafuckin' winners! You wanna beer, E?"

Ethan smiled through his annoyance at Barry's drunken behavior.

"Naw, I'm cool without drinking tonight man. Let's go in the house so I can see what kind of party you got going here."

"Yeah Man!" Barry screamed. "Excuse us, coming through. Pardon me, people. Move out of the goddamn way!"

The two young men entered the house like celebrities. Ethan began the ritual shaking hands and hugging babes like a politician. Then everything seemed to stop he saw her across the room. She turned to meet his gaze as if summoned. Oblivious to those around him, Ethan moved under a power not his own.

"I told you I'd try to make it." He said, grinning.

She returned his playful look, giving him a mirror into his own expression.

"It's really loud in here. Would you like to take a walk?" She startled him by saying the words he'd just formulated in his mind.

"Uh, yeah. Yeah, I'd love to."

In an instant, they were alone, walking down the street lost in the tranquility of the night. Ethan broke the silence.

"What made you come to Skyline?"

With a sparkle of life in her eyes she replied, "Love! I'm on a mission to understand it. The art of passion and how it relates to form connections."

Ethan was impressed and almost at a loss for words. "Have you been in love before?" He asked.

"Oh, there are a lot of different definitions for that. I know for me, love is life and what life has to offer. Love is being in the story of existence and feeling my connection to it."

"You sound as though you've learned the secret to life," he said with a hint of sarcasm.

She laughed. "There is no secret to life, only answers you don't have questions for. If there were a secret to living, then everyone would be dead until they figured it out. Don't you think?"

He considered her statement with skepticism. It didn't make sense. He had to ask, "Why would we be dead if there was a secret to life?"

"Don't you see? If there was a secret to being alive, then how could we exist? The secret of life… Just as a man and a woman create life, so do the earth and sun. What's the secret? There has been nothing hidden. It's right in front of our eyes. Even if we don't like how we are living that doesn't mean we are not."

The noise of the party brought Ethan out of his thoughts and back to the moment. They had rounded the block and were only a few houses away from Barry's. Ethan wondered if he had walked this route on his own intentions, or had he made a mistake in direction? He looked into Rio's eyes and none of that mattered. All he wanted now was to kiss her. He leaned in to sample the sweetness that he so desired, when she shattered his expectations yet again,

"My step-dad's here! I have to go. I'll see you at school Monday."

She was gone, and his cravings were left unsatisfied.

Standing on a cliff at the edge of the world with Rio by his side, Ethan knew what he had to do. He took her hand and they jumped. They jumped into the light. Falling and falling without end, and right before they reached the brightest part of the universe, they began to fly. Ethan awoke to the loving sound of his mother's voice.

"Ethan, wake up honey. You overslept. Barry is on his way over for your weekend jog." Her face offered warmth and love, a vision he welcomed all the time.

"Thanks, Mom."

"Oh, it's no problem honey. I'll have a nice big breakfast ready for you boys by the time you get back."

"Mom, I don't know what I'd do without you."

"Oh, I know what you'd do. You'd starve to death and sleep all day."

They shared a light-hearted chuckle. It felt good to hear his mother wrapped in the happiness of laughter, her smile a timeless image etched into his mind. It was the perfect time to ask,

"Mom, will you be free the Friday after next? We're playing the Knights and they have this free safety that's like a shark! He had my only interception of the season in our last game with them. I'm going to need all the support I can get. Will you be there?"

His mom's smile vanished, leaving only a somber expression. She averted her eyes as she would always do before delivering heartbreaking news to her little boy. "Isn't your father going to be there?" She asked moving toward the door.

Like a little boy afraid to let his mommy out of his sight, Ethan cried out, "Mom, don't be like that! Don't put me between you and Dad! We're a family. You're my mother and he's my father. Why can't I have you both there?"

Her eyes frantically searched the room but could find no escape from the reality of the moment. Tears welling in her eyes, she quickened her pace for the door. "You don't understand Ethan! This is not my fault. Now get ready for your jog. I've got to get back to the kitchen." Ethan thought to give chase but decided against it.

"Mom, I'm going out for my jog now. Do you want anything while I'm out?"

"No, honey. I have everything I need. Breakfast will be ready when you get back."

"Alright, I'll have my phone on me in case you think of something. I love you Mom."

"I love you too, honey."

Ethan's heart ached with thoughts of his mother's pain. He had to solve this problem.

"Dude, my head feels like someone is beating it with a hammer," Barry said as Ethan stepped out onto the porch. It was a beautiful day. The air was fresh, the birds in their morning song, and the sun shining brightly in the clear blue sky.

"You shouldn't drink so much if you don't want your head to beat like that!" Ethan snorted in a nasty tone. "You don't know when enough is enough, Bear. That's stupid, man. You have the chance to be a great football player, but you take it as a joke."

Ethan took off running. Barry followed, wanting to respond to Ethan's comment but what could he say? He changed the conversation.

"Man, E, that chick you left with was hot. Where did you meet her at?"

For the first time that day Ethan thought about Rio; his new inspiration in the operation of a kingdom.

"She goes to our school, Barry! I can't believe you haven't noticed her, man. You are not paying very good attention to your surroundings. You should be aware of the things involved in your life. She's probably seen you a helluva lot of times, knows who you are, and where you live, but you know absolutely nothing about her. How does that sound?"

"Damn, E, you're biting my head off this morning. I can't do nothing right in your eyes, dude. What's wrong? If you don't want to hang with me, then just say it. You don't have to slowly push me out. No matter what, I can take it if that's what you want but just let me know bro. What's up?"

Ethan was fully aware he'd been too hard on his friend, but in that moment, he didn't care. A dilemma that constantly perplexed him.

"Man, Bear, I just want you to do what's right. I see so much in you that's good, yet you do some stuff that's beneath your character. I watch you sometimes and get really upset because I know you're capable of so much more. I wish you would start living up to your potential. If I snap at you like I don't enjoy your company, then man I'm sorry for giving you that impression, that's not what it is. I just see a whole lot more in you than you're putting out. Do you feel me?"

Barry was touched by his friend's kind words. It was a rare

occasion for Ethan to pass out concern.

"Yeah, I feel you man. I'm going to try and stop drinking all together. I've wanted to do it and I just haven't been able to commit to it. If you could, I'd really like your help with it."

"Man, you got it, Bear! Don't even give that a second thought. I got you one hundred percent."

"Thanks, man. Thanks."

The two ran in silence the rest of the way, each in their own world, headed in different directions on these twisted roads of life.

Ethan's phone startled him with a buzz and a curious text message, *'Meet me tonight at the lake, eight o'clock.'* He didn't recognize the number and there wasn't any identifying reference. He texted back, *'Who's this?'* but received no response.

Breakfast and the rest of the day went by in a blur. He was so excited by the possibility of meeting Rio that everything else was unimportant.

Night consumed the day in an exchange so smooth Ethan hadn't even noticed. He grabbed his keys and made his way out the front door with the excitement and anticipation of an unknown encounter. He reached the lake at almost seven o'clock and chose a different tree to perch from, surveying the landscape. His heart pounded with excitement over the anticipation of possibly seeing her. Lustful thoughts of gratification consumed him. Why else would she choose to meet him at the lake tonight?

Finally, her silhouette cast its shadow over the path. It was almost 7:30, which thoroughly impressed him. She was early. He couldn't wait any more and prematurely jumped down from the tree and into the pathway of... Denise? Her face showed fury while he couldn't hide his surprise.

"Ethan, you're a fucking jerk! You used me to get yourself another girlfriend. Why couldn't you just be honest with me? Why, Ethan? What did I do to you?"

She broke down in sobs. Ethan paused wondering what happened.

He quickly regained himself without Denise being the wiser.

"Niecey, why do you think I used you?" He moved to comfort the trembling girl.

"You don't think I saw you two leave Barry's party? I have feelings, Ethan, and that was not right!" She screamed out like a hurt little girl. He embraced her tightly, wrapping his arms like a python around prey, smooth and easy. She began to relax.

"Niecey, do you think I could ever stop loving you?" His question pierced her thoughts, erasing her insecurities and leaving only his mark. Her defenses had been lowered.

"You know that I could never do that. Why would you even say it, or think it Niecey? You helped me build this! How many people have a connection like us? We shouldn't even have to speak to understand each other. If you want me to go away so you can be happy, then I will, but only if you want me to. What's up Niecey?"

He knew she didn't want him to go away. Her heart was hurt. She didn't know how to respond, she blurted out, "Well, what were you doing with her when you left the party? Why did you guys leave like that?"

Ethan looked at her, puzzled. "Why didn't you ask her before you came to me?"

"I'm not talking to that backstabbing bitch! I can't believe she left with you like that. She knows how I feel about you."

Ethan's face shifted from soft to stern revealing a look of bad taste in his mouth. He broke their embrace, leaving the cold night air in his place.

"How are you gonna tell a perfect stranger our personal business? You can tell her what you want about you, but don't tell her about me! That's hella weak Niecey. Hella weak! I don't want anything weak around me!"

Ethan turned his back and walked off, knowing she would follow.

"Ethan! I'm sorry! I didn't tell her what we do I just told her that I liked you before we went to the party, and then she left with you.

That's it! I'm sorry." Crying without tears, her arms folded in a defiant defense, she could feel her heart reaching to him, subconsciously calling him back to her.

His anger grew with every second. She wasn't crying. There's were no signs of tears. She was acting. He slowly moved towards her. Her sobs getting louder as if to pull him in faster. Tired of her performance, he chose to end it. "You're gonna sit here and try to lie to me as if I'm a fool?" His voice was a low growl, "I told you that I can feel you, Niecey, why are you trying to play me?"

Persisting, she pleaded, "Ethan, I didn't mean to do anything against you. I really didn't."

"I know you didn't mean it, Niecey," Ethan's tone was soft again, pulling her back in from the cold of his rejection, "That's all you had to say, but don't try and play on my emotions. Don't ever try and do that! Come here."

She walked slowly toward him like a scolded child. His arms slinked back around her, pulling her into his warmth.

On Sunday morning Ethan was up before the sun. He dressed in the calm of dawn thinking about the night before with Denise. Her foolishness could have ruined everything. He did have a strong love for her, but not in the way she wanted. He viewed the affection he bestowed on her a type of duty and preservation, it was not born of lust. When he made love to her it was to satisfy her craving for him and quiet her rapacious teenage mind. It was his way of protecting her from those who would do them harm. She was smart, but not ready to enter the world alone. When she was ready, he would let her fly free, but for now she needed to be under his wing.

The Mustang roared to life in the quiet morning streets. With no one else on the road, he let the white horse flex its muscles and become one with the road. It felt good to be in control of such a powerful machine. The scenery became a blur as Ethan's eye focused on the horizon and all that existed was him and the road. With his speeds pushing a hundred miles an hour, Ethan's solitude was interrupted by a siren behind him. His heart pounded in his chest as his foot moved to press the pedal harder, knowing he could take the cop on the wildest chase he'd ever seen. The fantasy was fleeting, and Ethan slowed to a stop, chuckling as the familiar slender-framed officer approached.

"Damn it, Ethan! How many times do I have to tell you to slow down?" The officer said approaching the driver's side window.

"Officer Sheets, I'm sorry. I was just blowing off some steam. I'm a little tense about next week's game."

The officer's expression settled into a familiar look of support and sympathy.

"Look, Ethan," the officer said in a warm tone, "there are more constructive ways to blow off steam than racing through the streets. You're a smart kid. What happens if you lose control? What happens if Mrs. Fletcher forgets to take her medication and lies down in the street again? You must think like that, Ethan. This thing is not a toy. It can hurt somebody."

Ethan looked up at the officer with well-worn puppy dog eyes, silently pleading his ignorance to any wrong doing, a familiar tactic he'd used with others in authority "I'm sorry, Officer Sheets. If you want, I'll park my car right here and call my mother for a ride home."

"Oh no, Ethan, you don't have to bother your mother right now. You just slow down and use your head." The officer said backing away from the car. "Tell your folks I said, hello. I'll see you at the game, son. Drive safe."

"All right, Officer Sheets. I'll drive safer." With that, Ethan put the car in gear and pulled off, enjoying his celebrity status.

Ethan pulled into the hotel's parking lot a little earlier than expected; he was just in time to see his father walking out with his secretary, a woman Ethan had known all his life. Standing in front of a parked car, they did not notice the solo figure coming toward them as they fully embraced in a kiss. Ethan's heart felt wrenched in pain and disappointment. The feeling made its way down to his stomach, and he felt like all his insides were writhing in agony. He could not believe what he was seeing.

"How could you do this, Dad? How could you do this to your family?" His voice quivered in anguish.

The culpable couple turned to see the angry young man walking toward them.

"Son, you don't understand. This is a complicated – "

"Complicated? You don't know what complicated is, dad. Complicated is how your wife and son feel. Your whore is not complicated!"

Enraged, Ethan was oblivious to the small gathering of onlookers.

"You keep this slut and leave me and Mom alone. I don't ever want to see you again!"

Ethan ran back to his car, trying to block out his dad's voice pleading with him to stop. He burned rubber as he sped away from the couple and onlookers. He hoped his plan would work.

"Ethan!" A sensuous voice called out. "Ethan, can I talk to you for a minute?"

It was Rio. Ethan stopped the procession of his entourage in the school hallway. The group fell silent. All eyes turned to the beautiful young woman.

"What's up, Rio?" Ethan separated himself from the crowd.

"It's nothing really, but I'd like to talk to you alone."

"Fellas," Ethan shouted, "I'll catch up with you at lunch." He turned around without waiting for a response. The group began to disperse. "Is that better?" He asked, making sure she understood his power more than the question.

"Yeah, that's a little better. What I have to say might take a little while. Can we go somewhere?"

"It's cool with me. Let's go."

The two walked alone, capturing the attention of everyone they passed. Even teachers seemed interested in the star quarterback parading the new girl in school.

"Ethan, I really like you. You're a cool guy, but I don't think it's good for us to hang out."

The victorious smile faded from his lips. In his mind he cursed Denise. "Why isn't it cool for us to hang out?"

"Well, you're just too consumed by aesthetic ideas that are never going to give you completion. It's a bad direction and one I don't want to go in."

Ethan felt offended by her superficial judgement. "What are you talking about?"

She shook her head knowing she had struck a nerve in his vanity. The ugliness of his true face was showing. "Ethan, I'm not trying to attack you. I just can't be around somebody who is so absorbed in their own world, someone who looks for things outside themselves to give them meaning. You're caught in this rut fashioned out of your fears. The only people who form set routines are those afraid of change. You fear the unknown and you're letting that fear keep you from experiencing something new."

"Hold on just one minute, sweetheart! You don't even know me! You don't know what I do other than what I show you or you assume."

"That's exactly my point, Ethan! That's all anyone knows about you. What do you do for yourself when the crowd isn't looking?"

The school bell sounded, alerting students that passing period was over. Rio looked down the hall and said, "Cut school with me! Prove me wrong and let's leave together right now."

Ethan found himself at a loss, uncertain of his next move. He had never cut school before. His father used to always tell him, '*People who cut school are the losers in this society. You can't count on them for anything but abandonment.*' Abandonment! His father must have cut a lot of school.

"Yeah, let's cut school. I don't feel like being here anyway."

Her face lit up. "You won't be disappointed. We have to hurry. Come on."

The two made their break like convicts escaping prison. Rio moved like a skilled professional. She knew where to go; through the halls to a side door, outside to a parking lot through a hole in a fence and then outside school. Ethan felt uneasy; he looked over his shoulder and almost tripped as he followed Rio. Out of his element, the star athlete's heart raced. He had walked this street countless times, but not during school. He was stepping into a new world where familiar things took on a whole new hue.

Rio squeezed his hand. "We have to catch that bus."

"We should have taken my car, Rio. Why are we getting on a bus?"

"Where is your car right now Ethan? Do you want to go back through all we just went through and delay where we could go right now? It's up to you, just let me know what it's gonna be, backwards or forward?"

She was right. Going back for his car would be a waste of time. After all, his car was locked up tight on school grounds. They'd take the bus, something else he had never done before.

"All right, let's get on the bus. But I gotta be back for football practice."

She laughed. "You think I want the whole school after me for making their star quarterback miss practice? You'll be back on time."

The bus seemed crowded for the middle of the day. Ethan cringed as a strong musky odor stung his nose. Rio did not appear to be affected by the scent. Ethan tried to avoid the eyes of a homeless man who was holding tight to a trash bag that had seen better days and averted his gaze from the woman breastfeeding her child. As Ethan cringed by all the noticeable things around him, Rio seemed excited to be on the bus.

"Where are we going?" Ethan inquired, taking a seat.

Rio smiling, "It's a surprise. Are you okay with surprises?"

Ethan smirked and said nothing. The bus lurched forward. A little over an hour passed dropping off people and picking people up. Ethan slipped off into a light sleep.

"It's the end of the line. Bus terminal!" The driver shouted.

Ethan woke finding himself in the city. This was where his father worked when he wasn't away on business. Where, as a boy, the man would bring his little prince and parade him around for the world to see.

"I really don't like the city that much. Why are we here?"

Rio gazed at him quizzically, as if to see where his troubles lay. She took his hand, gently guiding him. "We won't be here long, Ethan. I only want to show you one thing. If it's too much for you, we can get back on the bus and go back."

Go back, he thought. *No going back*. Rio's innocence penetrated his reflections. How could he refuse her harmless request? "All right, let's go and see this one thing you want to show me in the city."

In the joy of their newfound agreement Ethan and Rio exited the bus smiling. Everyone they passed seemed to be touched by their energy. The spirit of the young couple showed the world around them how something old can be rediscovered and reborn. A living definition of trust, Ethan held Rio's hand as she wove them through the current of moving people downtown. Ethan relaxed in her wake, a huge grin spread across his face, appreciating Rio's fluid movements through the crowd.

"How much further?" He asked, as if he weren't having fun, smiling from ear to ear.

"Come on Ethan, stop acting so uptight. We're almost there."

The couple walked a few more blocks before stopping at a coffee shop. This place was different from the franchises that dotted most of the city corners. The people working did not wear uniforms. Usually Ethan's first judgement would be to see these kinds of people as lazy pot smokers who lived off the fat of the land and still managed to complain about the weight they had to carry. It was his father's philosophy which Ethan had assumed about these types of people.

"Aye, Rio!" The warm greeting was from a long-haired guy sitting alone in a corner in front of a chess game in progress. Ethan felt strongly that this was a place that he did not want to be.

"Rio, what are we doing here?"

"Look!" She pointed in the direction behind the cash registers, and coffee makers. "This is why I brought you." His mouth fell open and his heart picked up pace. On the wall hung a mural of a football player wearing Ethan's jersey. He was running toward an end zone engulfed in flames. Decomposing bodies lay in his path. Bullets flew at the player from the fiery end zone. Instead of a football, the man cradled Earth in his arms. Behind the fiery end zone, the universe lay vast and deep.

"Do you like it?" Rio asked enthusiastically.

The hippies, the stench, the whole coffee shop fell into darkness around him. Ethan could only see the image on the wall.

"You don't like it, huh?" She said, lowering her face.

"Oh no, that's not it. I've never seen anything like it before. Who did it?"

"I did! I started working on it after I saw you at practice. I toured the campus a few times during the summer and that's when I saw you for the first time. That was before we met in class."

His heart skipped. She had noticed him before that day in social studies class and seen him well enough to create a massive mural. What did that mean?

"I've – I've never had anything this big done about me before. I like it. It's really nice. Thank you."

Sliding his arms around her and pulling her into the full warmth of his body's embrace, he held her tightly, enjoying the softness of her body. Time stood still as he tasted her mouth for the first time. The sweetness of her tongue and the softness of her lips overwhelmed his senses. He was completely lost in the kiss.

She pulled away. "We need to see one more thing. Let's catch a cab to the park."

Still floating, "Yeah, whatever you want!" He replied.

In the cab Ethan held Rio's hand, watching the city's changing sights. Strangers moved about everywhere, rushing to unknown destinations as if each was a life or death situation. Buzzing around in a million directions, no one really seemed to care about one another.

"Ethan," Rio purred, gently squeezing his hand, "do you believe in the stop light?"

"I'm not sure I know what you mean."

"Do you think the stop light is necessary for people to cross the street?"

"Well, without the stop light people would crash into each other and nobody would know when to stop and go. Plus, pedestrians would always be in the way, possibly even getting injured."

"So, you don't think that people can function together without some type of organized control?"

"I didn't say that. All I said was that without stop lights there could be a lot of confusion."

"Do you think that's right?"

"Do I think what's right?"

"Do you think that people should be dependent on things outside of themselves in order to interact together?"

Was she trying to upset him? Where was it coming from?

"Rio, people are dependent on things outside themselves every day, food, water, etcetera. it's just the nature of our world. We utilize the instruments and expand the boundaries of how far we can go."

She let go of his hand and looked away. "That's what I mean, Ethan. I shouldn't have kissed you."

He reached for her, but she pulled away.

"I don't understand. Why are you mad at me Rio? Look at me."

She did as he requested only to show puddles of tears in her eyes. "You're going to leave me because you don't understand. You think that everything is as simple as sight and sound, but that's not true. That's not love."

"What I don't understand, Rio, is your question on stop lights. How you can determine the future of our relationship on a question that means absolutely nothing!"

"*STOP THE CAB!*" Rio reached for the door handle throwing the fare at the driver and bolted from the car. Ethan found himself frozen in fury. He wanted to go after her but wondered if it was best.

"You still going to the park, buddy?" The driver said, as though he hadn't heard what just happened.

"No, I'm cool right here."

"That's a good move, buddy. Sounds like you got a winner. Good luck!" The driver said pulling away.

In a fog Ethan stood in place with no idea where to go. He scanned the moving people, hoping to find some sign of his love. Then in the distance he saw her standing near a man playing a guitar.

He rushed to her.

"Rio, what are you doing?"

She was smiling as if the episode in the car had not happened.

"I really like this song. My mother used to play it on the piano when I was a little girl." She reached in her pocket, pulled out a dollar, and dropped it in the musician's open guitar case. With the same hand, she took Ethan's. "Can we walk the rest of the way to the park?"

"Yeah Rio, whatever you want."

They walked in silence. Surrounded by the bustling energy of the city, all Ethan could hear was his breath. Stopping at a crosswalk, Ethan noticed the sign, *Don't Walk*. Cars flew through the intersection without hesitation. Pedestrians waited patiently for the sign to change. Ethan looked at Rio, squeezing her hand. They jumped into the intersection, trusting that the cars would not touch them. Moving swiftly, watching the flow of traffic, they dodged the cars adeptly and were on the other side of the busy, four-lane street before they knew it. Beaming with excitement, Rio grabbed him and passionately kissed him.

"I love you, Ethan. You understand now."

Ethan looked deep into her sparkling hazel eyes. "Yes, I do. It feels good. Thank you, Rio. I love you too."

The park was filled with the same hippie types as the coffee shop. A bunch of people with no shoes and unkempt hair. Everyone seemed lost in their own world. Ethan and Rio entered the park unacknowledged until a man yelled out.

"Chipmunk! What brings you back down to these parts?"

"Aye Rio!" A girl wearing sandals, shorts, and hooded sweatshirt sat braiding beads into another girl's hair.

"Rio, Rio," a scruffy, fat guy chanted from a circle of people passing cigarettes around. "I got one for you. Stop by before you leave."

"Alright, Jerry."

Ethan frowned seeing all these people he considered rejects of society jockeying for the attention of his girl. This was a place he would have never gone himself, and yet here he was.

"Come on, Ethan. There's someone that I want you to meet." Rio beckoned. She led him past all the people absorbed in their various activities to a tent tucked behind bushes in a remote area of the park.

"Shadow! Shadow!" Rio called out. "It's Chipmunk. I have someone I want you to meet."

A slow rustling inside the tent alerted them that her call had been heard. They stood silent, waiting. The zipper on the tent moved. Ethan felt like turning and walking away. He had no idea what to expect. Finally, a man emerged. He looked something like a voodoo priest. There was something regal about this man and Ethan felt a sense of honor being in his presence.

"Chipmunk," the man said in a deep, starchy voice sending waves through Ethan's body. "I see that you are in love. You are finally able to see this wonderful world. This young man marks the end of your adventure. His reflection can free you of the curse that plagues you. Enjoy the company of this young man. He has a lot to teach you about love, but your time together will be short. Go in peace."

The man went back into his tent leaving Ethan confused and Rio shaken.

"What was all that about?"

"Nothing Ethan, it was nothing. Let's go, we have to get back to school."

"No. Hold on a minute. Something is going on and I'm not going anywhere until I find out what it is!"

Rio could see the determination in Ethan's expression. Understanding his resolution, she sighed deeply and began.

"Ethan, my life is very different from yours. My family believes in things that you may not understand. Shadow is like our guide and I needed him to tell me if our union is meant to last. I've never been in love before and I had to consult him to find out if this feeling was okay. Do you understand? I'm in love with you Ethan and I barely know who you are."

Rio's words intrigued Ethan, but her reliance on the opinion of a man living in bushes, and the world in which she lived troubled him.

"Rio, I don't understand why you need someone outside of yourself to answer questions for which only you know the truth. What troubles me most is what he said. How can he tell how long we're going to be together? He said our time together will be short. You just asked me about people relying on things outside themselves, are you taking what he said seriously?"

Tears fell from her eyes which seemed to search the ground for answers.

"Ethan," she sniffled, "I don't want to talk about my family or our beliefs right now. All I want to do is enjoy my time with you and leave this place. Will you come with me?"

She extended her hand, waiting for his answer. There was no need for words. Ethan took her hand. She wiped her tears away, and they went back into the park's more social surroundings.

In the park Ethan did his best to have a good time. He laughed on cue and spoke when necessary, feeling like a clown performing for an audience. Ethan wore his mask well, but underneath, his confusion and curiosity took hold. He struggled to understand this strange girl he was with. He contemplated this creature and what her upbringing was like, who her family was, and why they placed a homeless man's opinion on a pedestal. He thought back to that morning in the motel parking lot with his dad. After all, who could understand family problems better than he?

"Ethan, we better go so you can be back on time."

"Oh, it's already time? It was nice meeting all of you. I hope to see you again soon." Familiar words that rolled off Ethan's tongue like a song he had sung many times.

"Yeah, we'll see you guys later," Rio replied.

Ethan was relieved to be leaving the park. He wanted to talk to

Rio by himself. A question had been burning in him. "Rio, what made you ask me about the stop light?"

She looked past him as if he hadn't spoken a word. "There goes our bus. We better hurry so we can get good seats."

Holding hands, they ran to the stop. A line to board had already formed, but Rio ignored the people already waiting and led Ethan to the front as if the other people weren't there. Some looked on angrily but didn't say a word as the couple got on the bus.

"Ethan, there are those who have become dependent on organized control and that's why they panic during a moment without organized direction. Without the stoplight, they're afraid. Hiding behind fear protects them from vulnerability and allows them to become self-absorbed.

"Very few people think of utilizing the stoplight as a tool. They allow the stoplights to take control and follow blindly. If all four lights go green, there is a 99% chance an accident will occur. They have no idea why they do what they do because they've become slaves to a tool."

"Come on, honey," Rio said smiling, "Let's sit over there."

Led by his love, they took their seats.

"'*Always be where you're beautiful*,' Shadow tells us. I'm glad you got to meet him. He's a wonderful teacher."

"Who is he, Rio?"

"Reflection. We listen to him for reflection."

"How does your family know a person like that?"

"Ethan, what if we are all sleeping and everything we experience is only a dream?"

"What are you talking about, Rio?"

"A being of pure energy is only one small part of a larger whole. The only separation from the whole comes in the form of this dream, which lasts a lifetime. Imagine being born into a dream, developing inside the dream and when your life is over, you wake up back inside the whole of reality.

"However long it takes you to go back to sleep does not matter because a thousand of our years is only a second to the universe. Once you do go back to sleep you can become whatever you want: a fish, a bird, a human, a tree, you can even become a star, or a comet, or a planet. The energy that causes decay is also what causes you to wake up. Without dreams, there can be no universe. Do you get it? I'll see you tomorrow at school."

She leaned over and gently kissed him on the cheek, bringing him back to reality. and the sound of the school bell ringing. They were back at the bus stop where their adventure had begun.

"How are you going to get home? I'll drive you if you need a ride."

"It's okay honey, I'm cool right here. I'll be alright, this bus is going my way. You should hurry before the driver gets mad and makes sure you're late for practice." Ethan noticed the driver looked irritated. He kissed Rio once more and jumped off the bus, making his way to the field for practice.

When he got home after practice, Ethan was eager to sleep and get to tomorrow, but his mother had dinner prepared for him. In no mood to eat, he washed up and sat down to dinner with his mother.

"How was school, honey?"

He hadn't been there all day and hated lying to his mother.

"Could you pass the potatoes, Mom?"

She did so with a curious look.

"You know how school is, Mom. It's the same thing every day."

His Mom giggled a bit. "Ethan. I know you weren't in class today. I saw your English teacher Mrs. Crosby at the market and she asked if you were alright. It took me by surprise, but I told her you were fine, and you'd be at school tomorrow. I'm not sure if she was aware of my initial shock, but your secret is safe with me. I'll write you a note so you can be cleared for your absence. I was a kid once, Ethan. I understand the need for adventure, but let's not make a habit of this."

Ethan had never known his mother to be this understanding. In fact, he had never known her reaction to these things at all. His father was usually the one who did the talking in these situations. His mother always deferred the punishment and judgment to him.

"Thanks, Mom. I'm sorry for lying to you. I was with this girl today and she's so different from other girls. You know?"

She laughed. "The ones you fall in love with usually are. Tell me more about her, honey. Do I know her?"

"No, you don't know her. She's not from around here. Mom, she looks at the world so differently to me and today I saw a world that I would never have seen before. She has this trip with how society is a mindless machine, controlled by instruments designed to make us mindless. I've never wanted to listen to anyone talk like that before, I usually just blow them off, but she's really different."

Ethan felt his mother's love through her warm and tender expression.

"Oh honey, when you are in love, things like that don't matter. There is no required type or ideal person for you to fall in love with. Just listen to your heart and examine how that person makes you feel. If her thoughts make you think, what does that mean? Explore your feelings as you get to know her habits and traits. Find out what makes you care about her, and the answer of whether you should be together will become clear. Do you understand, honey?"

"Yeah, Mom, I understand. I'm glad that we talked. You really helped me out a lot. I'll clear the table."

"Yes, you will young man!"

They laughed, clearing the table together What can be closer than mother and child?

The sound of the doorbell prompted inquiring looks, neither of them expected company.

"I'll get it, Mom." If it was one of his friends they'd be in store for a big piece of his mind. How dare they interrupt him without warning at this hour.

"Who is it?" Ethan shouted.

"It's me, son." A voice replied. Ethan looked at his mother for approval and, with a nod, she gave her okay.

"What brings you here this late, Dad? Shouldn't you be having dinner with your new family?"

The typically proud man hung his head low. "I guess I deserve that one. There's nothing I can say that will make what I've done right. I just came here to talk to your mother."

"Why would you want to do that now?" Ethan snapped back. "I don't know why she'd ever want to see you again. I don't want to see you. You should see if you can still catch that dinner with your new bride, Dad."

"Ethan," his mother shouted, "it's alright. Let him in."

"Mom, how are you going to let him in here after what he's done to us?"

"Ethan," she said more sternly. "It's alright. Let him in."

With anger in his eyes the young man stepped aside, allowing his father to enter. The older man walked in with his head still bowed. As soon as he crossed the threshold the front door closed so hard the house shook. This was followed by the sound of Ethan's Mustang tearing away from the house.

"Barry! Barry!" Ethan yelled outside his friend's window. "Barry!"

The window opened. "What's going on, E? What are you doing here so late?"

"I need a place to crash tonight. Is it cool or what?"

"Yeah dude, it's cool. Wait right there. I'll be down in a sec."

Ethan stared at the night sky, wishing he could escape reality. He wanted his parents back together, yet maybe they were better off apart. No matter what, his father needed to be punished for his betrayal. Ethan could not allow his father's actions to be swept under the rug as though they had never happened. A person must repay their debt to the hearts that have been betrayed, before asking to be forgiven.

"What's the deal, E? My parents are having a cow about my grades and your being here will only add to the problem. Let's shake the spot for a while and cruise around, dude. You down?"

"Yeah, I'm down with that. Let's go!"

The two boys jumped in Ethan's car and rode out with the music low and no particular destination in mind.

"Aye, E you wanna go to the lake and chill for a minute."

"Yeah! That sounds cool, Bear. Is anybody raging there tonight?"

"There might be some people there. You remember that dude, Jake, who lost his scholarship for selling pot?"

"Oh yeah. He was the first-string varsity quarterback when we were freshmen. What ever happened to that dude?"

"Man, E, that dude is bad news now. He's got a whole bunch of losers he hangs with and he's been in and out of jail since he lost his scholarship. He's probably gonna be there tonight with his crew, but they usually have a whole bunch of older chicks there. So, it should be cool."

"Bear, you sound like you've been there with them before?"

"Yeah, I bought some pot from him for my party and he had me meet him there."   "You've been smoking pot, Bear?"

"Naw, I haven't been smoking. It was for some chicks. You know how they get off on that stuff, man. So, I scored some, but when I offered it to the chicks, they turned me down. I was kinda mad because one of the girls I offered it to is a straight burn out. Get this, Dog! She was trying to quit. The night I got action at scoring, she's cool on smoking! And she had to go home early."

Ethan laughed. "Man Bear, you got all round bad luck when it comes to the ladies. Who was she?"

"Burn out Rachel."

"Oh yea, burn out Rachel is a freak for some weed, Bear! Last time I saw her she was looking for fat Freddie."

"She was? Aw man, I'm gonna have to give her a call now. I still got that pot I scored."

The two boys were laughing hard as they enter the parking lot for the lake. Several cars were there already. They had found a party on a weekday.

"E! Act like you're already high so we don't look like a bunch of lame-o's to the older chicks."

Ethan looked at Barry like he was crazy.

"Man, we don't have to impress chicks like that. They will be impressed with how cool we are. Man, Bear, what's wrong with you? Do you know who you're with?"

"E, these chicks aren't like that, man. They're older. They don't care that we're high school football stars."

"Man, Bear, just follow me and watch my lead."

Barry shook his head and shrugged his shoulders as he followed Ethan through the entrance to the park. The chill in the air raised the hair on their arms, but the sound of laughter began to warm them up with the anticipation of something new. The way Barry thought they needed to pretend to be high to hang out with some cool chicks. *Crazy,* Ethan thought.

"What's up, Jake?" Ethan said walking into the crowd.

Jake stared at Ethan as though he had been insulted. The crowd fell silent with the introduction of the two strangers. The tension grew as everyone stood there watching.

"Do I know you, man?" Jake said focusing on the young boy even more.

"Yeah!" Ethan replied defensively, "we used to play football together."

Jake stared harder until his frown became a smile.

"Yeah, I do remember you. You're that kid who went all-state last year. You were junior varsity when I was there. What are you doing here on a school night, kid?"

"Oh, we were just looking to hangout and relieve some stress. Nothing too big."

Jake let out a laugh, "Kid, you're in the wrong place for that. We ain't trying to get caught babysitting some young punks. You two go find somewhere else to relieve some stress."

Clearly offended, Ethan lowered his brow trying to figure out where the disrespect was coming from. He moved in closer, walking two or three steps toward Jake before saying,

"Look man we came to the lake to hang out. Now if you're gonna be a bitch about it, then we're cool with you, but we ain't leaving the lake because you said so."

Jake seemed to take Ethan's defensiveness in stride, masking his own offense with a chuckle. "Aw, look everybody, the little boy wants to play." The tense group no longer silent began to giggle. "Alright quarterback boy, you can hang, it's cool."

Ethan wasn't used to people laughing at him, and he wasn't going to allow it to go unpunished. "Hold on man. Who are you calling a boy? You can't tell me when or where to do nothing. You're nothing!"

Ethan swung, hitting Jake hard in the face. It was clear after a few blows that Jake was no match for the star athlete. Under the rain of punches Jake pulled something to even the fight. A piercing pain shot through Ethan's abdomen into his back. Screams erupted from all around him. A bright light flashed in the night, then all Ethan could see was red and blue lights, and shadows moving everywhere.

"It's the cops! It's the cops!" A woman's voice screamed out. Barry's face came into focus, obscuring the flashing lights and fleeing shadows. Ethan blacked out.

"Doctor Katz, please report to the E.R." With unusual effort, Ethan opened his eyes. He saw his mother sleeping in a chair by the foot of the bed, and tubes running from various parts of his body. It was too much to process. He forced himself back asleep.

Rio was standing next to Jake. Ethan called to her, with no response. He ran toward her, she had to know she was in danger, but the faster he ran the further away she stretched. She took Jake's hand and yelled, "I never loved you Ethan!"

Ethan's throat was dry when he woke to the sun piercing his eyes. Alone in his room he tried to sit up, but the pain was too much. A fool's punishment for attacking a thug. He'd acted in such a lowly and undignified manner. In frustration he grabbed the button by his bed to call for a nurse.

A cheerful woman enters the room. "Hello there, you're awake! Your family and your girlfriend are still here. All sorts of people have been calling to see if you're ok. You're a big celebrity around here! I'm going to need to help you to sit up, so I can look at your wound."

Ethan was still trying to process what was happening, the path he normally walked had been severely altered.

"You said my girlfriend is here?" His dry, raspy voice was moistened with the taste of his own sweet blood.

"Don't try to speak too much right now. You've been out for almost twenty hours. Yes, your girlfriend is outside with your mom and dad. They'll be in here shortly. Oh, this wound needs to be cleaned. I'm going to have to change these bandages."

The cleaning solution burned like hot coals pressed into already angry wounds. Ethan forced his mind to drift to his sweet Rio manifesting herself from the heavens so that she could be with him at this moment.

"Alright," the nurse said, pulling him from his trance. "All done. Now I'm going to let your family come in here to see you. They can't stay long because you need your rest. I'll be back in a second." The impenetrably perky nurse left the room.   "Dude," Barry said as he ran to Ethan's side. "Man, I was worried you were gonna die. The cops got that dude Jake and he is in jail where he belongs. I told them everything. I can't believe what he did man. I'm sorry for asking you to go there. How do you feel bro?"   Ethan heard his friend's question, but his eyes were locked on his love.

"Are you alright, E?" Barry said with growing concern.

"Yeah, yeah, I'm fine Barry.... just a little sore. Did I get him good before he stuck me?"

"Dude, it all happened so fast, but you were whooping him; he only hit you one time. I came rushing in when I saw him pull the knife, but by the time I got there he took off running. The cops were quick on the scene like somebody had already called. Dude ain't cool for that, E."   "Yeah," Ethan sighed. "That wasn't cool what he did, but I was stupid for trying to fight him. Should have just walked away. I almost lost my life." He swallowed the silence as the depth of his admission sunk in. His love walked closer to be by his side.

"I'm just glad you're okay," she said reaching over and grabbing his hand gently. "When I heard what happened I was scared that you were going to die. I don't know what I would have done if I lost you." She sat on the bed and rested her head on his shoulder, her sobs muffling on his neck.

Aware that the lovers wanted to be alone, Barry stood up. "I'm going to grab something to eat. Do you guys want anything?"

"Naw, man," Ethan replied, holding Rio close with one arm.

"We're cool bud, thanks."

"It's no problem, E, it's no problem. I'll be back in a minute."

The door closed leaving the couple in the room alone.

"I'm alright, sweetheart, I'm alright." He assured her, stroking her hair as the intensity of her cries increased.

"Ethan, you just don't know how much you mean to me. Last night I felt you. I knew that something was wrong. I called your house and your Mom told me that you were gone, and she didn't know when you'd return. I told her it was important that I talk to you and asked that she please tell you that I called. When I told her my name, she promised you'd get my message as soon as she talked to you. I sat alone in my room waiting for your call. As the endless hours passed I fell asleep for a few moments and awoke to a pain in my back that wouldn't go away. I called your house again and your father answered. He told me there had been an accident. I was so scared, baby. The pain in my back still won't go away."   Her head drifted from his neck to his chest where her tears stained his hospital gown. His actions had caused this. How could he have been so stupid? The door opened slowly as Ethan's parents entered. Barry came in behind them and gently pried Rio from Ethan's chest. Ethan watched his love, wondering why Barry was taking her away, without question. Something was wrong.

"I'm sorry, honey," Ethan's dad said to Rio, wiping a few tears from his eyes. "You two kids go get some rest and come back later."

Ethan wondered how many other tragic scenes had unfolded in this sterile room. How many had felt this impending fear?

"Alright, Mr. Smith," Barry said, "I'll take Rio home and come back later. Alright, E, rest up man."

Rio blew a kiss and waved softly. The door closed behind them. Ethan's father took a deep breath, his chest broadening as he spoke. "Ethan, how are you feeling?"

"I'm – I'm feeling fine, Dad. As a matter of fact, I was wondering when I can leave."

His Dad's lips pursed. "Son, you are very lucky. The blade of that kid's knife missed severing your spinal cord by only a few centimeters. You could have been paralyzed."

"Dad, tell me what's the problem? What's going on?"

The older man looked away, in a moment unable to face his son but slowly he brought his eyes back to his young prince. "Son, you were in surgery for a long time. The doctors did everything they could to relieve the pressure on your spine. It's a miracle that you'll be able to walk. There's no easy way to say this. The doctors say that you will never safely be able to play football again. Now that's not to say it's the end of the..."

Everything else from there moved in an inaudible slow motion. He heard his father's voice but couldn't comprehend his words. His mother's sobbing seemed far away. *You'll never be able to play football again*. The words echoed, as if repetition would make them comprehensible. *You'll never be able to play football again... You'll never be able to play football again! Why? Why?* He thought.

"Why?" He screamed out loud. A single tear crept down his father's face. "I'm sorry son, I'm sorry."

Ethan closed his eyes and for the first time in many years he prayed because he didn't know what else to do. He hoped that somehow, he would open his eyes and be in his bed at home. But sadly, when he opened them, the nightmare persisted.

On a sunny winter day Ethan found himself smiling, happy to finally be leaving the hospital. The doctors and nurses were amazed by his progress. He still had more physical therapy to undergo, but he was walking. Through sheer will and determination Ethan was able to walk, but he struggled with the notion that he would not regain the ability to play football. In the car, Ethan's mind drifted to memories of Rio and how she'd been with him at the hospital every day; reading to him, playing new music, keeping him up to date on the things happening at school. But most importantly, she was there sharing her love. The night he asked her to be his girlfriend her beauty had captivated him, and he was lulled by the song of her voice, barely able to understand the words for the melodic hypnosis he was under. Pulling himself from her siren song, he spoke more from his heart than he'd ever done. Her response was not what he expected.

"I already am your girlfriend! I don't understand."

By definition she was, so what was he asking her? He thought for a moment, investigating his intentions. He wanted her to be his and his alone. He uttered what was on his mind and the look on her face scared him. She seemed to pull back, a flash of fear dashed across her face.

"What?" He asked, "What's the problem?"

She smiled showing a deep understanding for Ethan. "Oh, honey, I'm not going anywhere. You don't have to worry about losing me. I'm not going to leave you."

"But will you be mine, Rio?"

She placed her hand over his heart. "Ethan, I have troubled your heart, which is something I never wanted to do. You must understand that love can never be yours to own. Love comes and goes like day and night. You and I both love many different things and in time we will love new things. For me to promise my love to you, for you to own, is something I cannot do. Right now, at this moment, I love you so much and I will be back tomorrow to love you some more. You don't need to place an official title on our relationship, honey. Our relationship is ours and there is no need to define it for others. Your relationship with someone else is your relationship with them."

He kissed her tenderly, as she smiled back, holding her secret safe, deep in her heart.

As his family drove him home from the hospital, Ethan found himself dwelling on his conversation with Rio. Fear caused him to relate his passion with ownership. He'd learned long ago that to love something was to possess it as his own. Yet again, Rio had shifted his consciousness and opened his mind to new ways of looking at the world around him.

"Well, we're home son," Ethan's dad remarked as he turned the car engine off. "Do you need help getting out of the car? Matter of fact, I'm not thinking. I'll help."

"I'm alright Dad, I got it." His dad's voice had refocused Ethan's mind on the situation at hand. Opening the door, Ethan stepped back into reality.

Sharp pains shot through Ethan's body as he struggled to get out of the car. Spurred forward by the sight of his house and the thought of his own bed, he stepped carefully, trying not to fall. His father walked close by, offering a sense of security that Ethan thought had been lost since that day in the motel parking lot. They stepped through the front door and, *"Surprise!"* Ethan's mind was fuzzy from the medication as he worked to process the scene before him. In his living room stood friends, family, some of his teachers, and in the center, Rio, her smile a beam of love reflecting all he felt inside for her. Buoyed by the warm reception of love and support from all who loved him, Ethan's energy picked up and he welcomed a momentary distraction from all the thoughts swirling though his mind.

After few hours that saw people coming and going, all welcoming him back home and wishing him a speedy recovery, Ethan was relieved that the evening seemed to be coming to an end. He wanted some time to be alone with Rio before she'd have to leave. It had been her idea to plan all of this for him. His mother who had been beside herself with grief yet overjoyed by his recovery, welcomed the idea and helped plan the party. Ethan found himself hypnotized, watching Rio help his mother clean. Every move she made seemed designed to entrance him.

"Rio." He called to her, feeling himself drawn toward her, but too exhausted to move.

"Yes, honey, what do you need?"

Goosebumps rippled up and down his arms in waves. She was so close. He could feel her breath tickle his face; smelling its sweet scent. He impulsively pulled her to him, kissing her soft, perfect lips. Lost in a moment he wished would never end, Rio pulled away. Her tender smile. In her eyes he thought he saw eternity.

"Rio, let's go outside for a minute."

She took his hand. "I'd go anywhere with you."

With some effort, Ethan took the few steps to the front porch. The wind howled, dominating the quiet street. Holding hands, they watched the fast-moving clouds change their forms overhead.

"I love you." He said quietly, still looking toward the sky.

"I love you, too." She said, looking at him.

Feeling a call, he turned to meet her eyes. The bliss he'd seen in them such a short time ago shifted to something dark and ominous. Where had the love of his life gone? Instead of the tender, caring person who'd spent days at his side, Ethan saw only confusion, betrayal, hatred and envy swirling in the windows to her soul, each dark emotion fighting for position and control. The smile he loved so dearly had been replaced as well. A devious look surfaced from deep within her. What was he seeing? He blinked to clear his eyes, hoping for the return of his love.

"Honey, is everything alright?"

"Everything is fine, honey. Why do you ask?" Her voice was almost begging for help. Her eyes teetered in transition.

"I – I don't know. I guess I'm still woozy from the medication or something. Never mind."

Looking inquisitively, her smile softened. "Ethan, why do you have to be so amazing?"

"Huh? I don't understand, Rio. What did I do that was so amazing?"

She leaned over to kiss him on the cheek. "You're so silly. You know what you did."

Ethan felt more lost than before. He didn't want to offend her, but he had to know. "Honey, I really don't know what you mean."

She smiled disarmingly at him then looked up into the sky. "You know what's funny, my love? Most people are afraid to admit certain things because they don't want to look or sound stupid to others. It's a phobia that paralyzes some people, trapping them in their own way of thinking. A world protected by walls of fear which imprisons rather than protects their thoughts. Once your thoughts are imprisoned, Ethan, you're as good as dead because your thoughts are what you are. So why be afraid of sharing your perception? Are your thoughts not good enough? Is it peer pressure? Or is it that you don't want to face the reality of what's on your mind?"

He was beginning to comprehend what she was saying but was still afraid to admit what he'd seen.

"Ethan," she said softly. "I'm asking you a question. What makes you afraid to speak your mind?"

The moment had become tense and challenging. Ethan searched his mind for the proper thing to say but was unable to find anything to satisfy her question. It was then that he realized his problem. "The thing that makes me not speak my mind freely is that, like most people, I'm considering other people's reactions and I'm constantly tailoring my words to fit that. My silence is not fear as much as trying to say the right thing."

Her laugh only served to increase the tension he felt.

"What's so funny? I was serious about what I said."

"Ethan, I'm not sure I was clear when I asked you that question. I do understand the need to consider other people's feelings when using your words, but what I meant was in regard to speaking your mind without fear of looking like a fool. You looked into my eyes a moment ago and saw my soul, but you denied what you saw. Did you think I would judge you for what you thought you saw?"

His heart skipped a beat. *How did she know?* "You… you know what I saw?"

"Of course I know, Ethan. I'm the one that showed you. One day you'll understand me better, but today is not that day. I love you."

She kissed him passionately and his mind was so engulfed by her that he didn't notice the car pull in front of the house. Before he knew what was happening, she was gone.

Beep, beep, beep… The alarm clock alerted Ethan that the morning had finally come after a long night spent tossing and turning, thinking about what Rio had shown him.

"Ethan, are you up yet? Honey?" The door opened, revealing his mother standing there, glowing. He had barely seen her smile recently, this was a welcome sight. "Ethan, is everything alright? You're looking at me as if you've seen a ghost."

"No, Mom, everything is fine. You just look happier than you have in the past few weeks."

Smiling she walked over and sat next to him on the bed. "Well, honey, things are getting better for me. I love your father very much and, believe it or not, he loves me too. We have a few problems that need to be worked out and we are working through them, but we need time."

Ethan's face soured at the mention of his father. The pain from his father's betrayal resurfaced. "Mom, Dad left us for his whore, and now we're supposed to accept him back as if he's done nothing wrong? That's not something I'm willing to do right now. You can let him back, but as far as I'm concerned, he's still gone."

"Ethan, he is your father and you will respect him as such! He loves you and what happens in my relationship with him should not interfere with the love you two have for each other. Is that understood?"

Ethan felt his mother's need for hope and he didn't want to take away her glow. He would not bring her pain like his father. "I'm sorry, Mom. I – I know that he is my father and I do love him, but what he did was not just directed toward you; it was directed toward us. He hurt me too, Mom."

Ethan's eyes burned with unexpressed pain, his tears boiling up from deep within. Unwilling to suppress them any longer, he let them pour down his cheeks. He was speaking his mind without fear of being a fool. It was a freedom he had not experienced in a long time.

"Come on, honey," his mom stood up, "you have to get ready for school. We'll talk more about this when you come home." She kissed him on the forehead before leaving the room.

Ethan dressed quickly and in moments was standing before his white horse. He and his beloved car had been apart for so long. He'd been pining for this moment; he savored opening the door. Ethan thought about how lucky he was to have such a car. Firing up the car's engine, he settled in his seat and grasped the wheel as the powerful machine roared to life.

At Barry's house with the car's top down and music blaring there was no need to honk the horn for, as always, Barry ran out and hopped into the passenger seat.

"What's up, E?"

"What's up?" Ethan greeted his friend as he put the car in gear and pressed the gas pedal, the force of horses pushing them back in their seats.

"Man, E, I have got to tell you something. That chick Denise is flipping out, man. She's bad mouthing you to anyone who will listen. She told Tiffany that she saw you shooting dope last summer with that dude, Jake, and that's probably the reason he stabbed you. Can you believe that? Why is she talking like that, dog? I thought you guys were cool!"

Ethan kept his cool, seeming unfazed as he processed the information. He knew it was his own error that caused this. He had driven Denise to this point by turning her into a cornered animal hissing and scratching at anything that came near.

"Aye, Bear, we're going to be a little late for school man. Got to make a stop somewhere first."

They arrived while class was in session. The campus was still, with only a few students wandering around. It was not the welcome Ethan had dreamed for his first day back in the kingdom, but he had to adjust his plan for his return. Some of his subjects had become unruly during his absence, so a silent arrival was required.

"Barry, I want you to meet me in front of the cafeteria at lunch. Round up all the guys and have them with you. Don't tell anyone I'm here."

Barry smiled at his friend. "It's amazing how your mind works, E. Like a mad genius or something. It's good to have you back, dog. See you at lunch."

Ethan watched his friend head off to class before getting out of the car and heading to the principal's office.

"Dominic," Ethan said quietly, surprising the awkward young man before him.

"Mr. Smith!" Befuddled, Dominic abandoned his task of fixing papers for the principle's secretary and turned to acknowledge his king. "How are you doing, sir?"

"I'm doing fine, Dom. I'm fine. I'm in a hurry right now, I need to talk to you about something."

"Anything you want, sir! What do you need?"

"I need you to clear me for all my classes today."

"All of your classes today, sir?"

"Yeah, Dom, I don't have time to explain. Just make sure I'm cleared for my absences."

"Alright, Mr. Smith, is there anything else I can do?"

"Yeah, there is something else you can do. I need you to call Rio out of class and excuse her for her absences too."

"Alright, Mr. Smith, I hope you're feeling better."

"Thanks Dom! I'm feeling better than ever right now. Tell Rio to meet me at my car."

"Alright Mr. Smith, sure thing." Without another word, Ethan walked off, feeling good to be back in his kingdom.

Rio appeared in his rear-view mirror like an apparition, floating toward him and his horse. Ethan found himself frozen in place, his breath caught in his throat, while his heart seemed ready to beat out of his chest. She opened the passenger door.

"Ethan, what are you up to? Dominic said to meet you out here and that I'm cleared for all my absences today."

He kissed her softly on the lips. "I was thinking about you, as I always do, when I realized that you've never rode in my white horse before."

She gave him a quizzical look. "What are you talking about, Ethan? What's your white horse?"

"My car!" He said with a laugh. "You've never ridden in my car before."

Now it was Rio's turn to laugh. "You named your car?"

"Yeah. What's wrong with that?"

"Nothing is wrong with it if you're a nerd. I never thought that a cool guy like you would name his own car." She laughed a little harder. Ethan tried to look serious, but her energy was infectious.

"That's it," he said, unable to continue the fight against his grin, "I'm going to show you what happens to people who laugh at the king!"

He grabbed her firmly by the waist as she tried to pull away, and with that they began to wrestle playfully. Always aware of his surroundings, Ethan gave a quick glance around the car to make sure their playing went unnoticed. Their bodies pulsed against each other, stimulating the chemistry of arousal. Two lovers laughing and giggling, wrestling for the dominant position. Catching each other's eyes, their laughter stopped and turned into hungry kisses. Ethan savored the sweet taste of her mouth, wishing he could become part of her.

His kisses brushed along her skin from her lips to her neck. He whispered in her ear, "Let's get more comfortable." They moved to the back seat. Slowly and gently he lifted her shirt moving down to kiss her beautiful stomach. Her soft flesh stimulated him in ways he had never experienced. Removing her bra, he exposed her breasts. They were more beautiful than he had imagined, as perfect as a painting. In her eyes, the innocence of a child gazed up at him, begging him to be gentle. He took his time removing his shirt to reveal his muscular build. She was his. He lowered himself down on top of her, the warmth of her body sending goosebumps up his spine. From her breasts he laid trails of soft bites and kisses back down to her stomach. Stopped by her pants, he pulled down her zipper and unbuttoned the waist revealing white, cotton panties with little black cat paws printed all over. He couldn't help smiling, thinking how cute it was that a woman with such a mature sense of self could wear such adorably youthful panties. Meeting eyes, she smiles knowing exactly what he's thinking. He tugged on the waist of her jeans and she lifted her body to help. With her legs exposed he admired her thighs, soft and plump, curving at the right points to stimulate his delight. A few more kisses on a new part of her body as he moved his hand toward her panties. Again, she lifted her body to aid his efforts. The sight of her pubic hair tantalized him as her sweet aroma filled him with an overpowering desire. He kissed his way up her inner thigh, drawn to this new destination. His tongue met her sweetness first. She let out a soft moan as she moved, pressing into him in a rhythm all her own. Her warm juice flowed into his mouth; and all he wanted was more. Using his lips, tongue, and fingers as the instruments to produce sounds of pleasure he searched for different notes to compose their unifying song.

Her moans sung higher and higher until he found it. The note of climax! Her warm flower pulsed, gushing sweet nectar into his mouth. Grabbing his head, she pressed his face into her vibrating pussy. Her entire body clinched and flexed uncontrollably, she finished with a trembling that resembled a seizure and with a final gush of nectar she screamed his name. Her grip on his head relaxed, followed by the rest of her body. He pulled his head away from this place she'd cum, admiring the beauty of this place now open like a flower in full bloom. He blew his cool breath from her stomach to her thighs as he pulled down his pants. Purring in pure ecstasy, she opened her eyes to see him putting a condom on. Biting down on her lip, she closed her eyes, and with a kiss he pressed himself into her. It was the moment they both had been waiting for.

After their sensational experience, they dressed, lost in separate thoughts.

"Ethan," she purred while pulling on her pants, "do I make you happy?"

Furrowing his brow in question he smiled.

"Of course, you make me happy. Why would you ask me that?"

"It seems like something's on your mind. It's the same thing I could feel when I first got into the car. I don't know what it is, but I know it's bothering you and I hope it's not me."

Ethan sighed heavily, pausing to choose his words carefully in the wake of their intimate encounter. "Honey, you always make me happy. What's bothering me is here at school, and that's why I called you out."

"What is it, baby? Can I help you? You know I'll do anything for you."

Taking her hand in his, the energy between them hummed. "I do need your help, babe. Denise has turned against me and has been attacking my reputation with lies that attempt to assassinate my character."

"What?"

"Listen. I don't want to fight with her. I want her to submit and admit to everyone that she lied because she was jealous and hurt. I want her to repent."

Burying her head into his chest, Rio agreed. "Yes, that is what needs to be done. We must make her honor your true power."

Her words lifted the weight Ethan had felt so heavily on his shoulders. He embraced her, inhaling her scent, and with her head against his chest Ethan felt a deep comfort in her agreement.

"Rio look at me," her beautiful eyes captured him. "I want you to talk to Denise. I want you to make her feel comfortable and bring her to me.

"That's all you need me to do?"

"Yes... that's it."

"Consider it done my love."

The sound of the lunch bell alerted him. The champion was ready to defend his title. The king and his queen exited their chariot and headed towards the arena.

Denise smiled smugly thinking about the rumors she'd started and how hungrily Ethan's so-called subjects had gobbled them up. As she entered the cafeteria she was thinking more about what to say than what to eat when a man she had never seen before stopped her.

"Miss," the man said, holding a bouquet of flowers, "these are for you."

Denise looked at them, confused. "Sorry, sir you have the wrong girl. Those are for someone else."

"The name on here says Denise," the man said. "I was told to find the prettiest girl on campus and deliver these to her. So here you go. There's a card inside." Denise took the flowers. "Enjoy your day," the man said before turning to leave.

"Who told you to deliver these to me? How did you know what I looked like?"

"The card will explain everything. Enjoy your day."

Denise stood in disbelief looking down at the two-dozen beautiful long-stemmed roses in her arms. Who could have sent them?

"Denise, you have a secret admirer?" Her friend Sheri asked, after witnessing the bizarre encounter.

"Sheri, I have no idea. It might be that guy Jason who's been asking me out lately. The delivery man said the card would explain everything."

"Well, what does the card say?"

"I don't know. I haven't read it yet."

"Well, what are you waiting for? Read it."

Denise took the card off the flowers and stepped out of the cafeteria to avoid any more attention.

"Well, what does it say?" Sheri asked impatiently.

Denise couldn't believe it.

"Who is it from, Niecey?"

"It's – It's from Ethan."

Denise's shock spread to her friend, who knew how Denise felt about Ethan.

"What did he say?"

Denise looked away in a feeble attempt to hide the shame spreading across her face. All the arrogance she'd felt from the power of her words drained from her as her face became pale.

"Sheri, I – I can't read this again. Take it. Please."

Sheri took the card from her friend's trembling hand it read, Niecey, I really miss you and want you to know I'm thinking of you. I hope these roses brighten your day as you always brighten mine. I can't wait to see you. Sincerely, Ethan.

Sheri put her arm around her friend who was now quietly sobbing with regret.

"It's gonna be alright, Niecey. Don't cry. Everything is gonna be fine now. When you get home, give him a call, and explain how hurt you were. He'll understand."

Sheri's words didn't ease Denise's burden. She would have to explain to people that she was wrong before he returned to school.

"Do you really think he'll forgive me?"

"I know he will, girl. He loves you."

"I have to fix this Sheri. Hold these flowers so I can fix my makeup."

Sheri took the flowers, admiring them in the light, when a shadow imposed darkness over them. Annoyed, the girls looked up to see Rio standing over them, smiling. Denise's breath caught in her throat as her insides clenched tight, anxious with anticipation about the meaning of Rio's presence in that moment.

Ethan's court gathered, having no idea he was approaching. His faithful court of merry men were enjoying another moment of simplicity, laughing and joking. Barry saw him first and shouted,

"E-Nut!"

The others turned around and moved towards him, "E-Nut! E-Nut!" Others joined, as the group circled their prized leader's return.

Students looked on as they passed by. A couple of sophomore girls turned their noses up at the spectacle. One of the boys, Rod, noticed the girls' display and jumped out of the circle, landing right in front of the girls, "Do you know who that is?"

The girls, startled by the large boy brazenly blocking their path, didn't say a word.   "Well, since you don't know who that is, I'm going to tell you. He's the reason why your school is the most feared in the state! He's the reason why we always have a reason to party! He's the reason why we're state champions! Go Spartans! Go Spartans! Go Spartans! Go Spartans! Go..."

Satisfied with frightening the girls he allowed them to move on but not before his cheer caught on like a plague, echoing in the mouths of others walking the halls. Ethan smiled knowing he was the cause of activity around him. Without a word, he began to walk, parting the group to make a lane. Once in front, the crowd followed behind their beloved hero, growing with people at every step. The herd was a rumble of laughing, talking, screaming and chanting; various voices meshed into a stadium-like roar similar to what he heard during one of his games.

Ethan was a proud leader taking his troops on parade to the site of his target. Three young women stood before him; watching him approach with the large crowd behind him. Two of the girls gasped while the third smiled knowingly. Ethan looked Denise directly in the eyes and frowned, shaking his head. All she could do was turn away.

"Rio," he called out. "Rio!"

The crowd fell silent at the sound of his voice and turned their focus to the girl blessed by his attention. He extended his hand and she moved towards him. As Rio approached and took Ethan's hand the whispers began. The couple raised their hands together as Ethan's voice boomed out, resurrecting the battle cry, "Go Spartans! Go Spartans! Go Spartans!"

The crowd erupted in cheers allowing their king and his queen to walk off, alone.

"You want me to drive you home?" He asked, opening the door to his trusty white horse. "No, thank you, love. I – I have somewhere else I have to be. Could you drop me off at the rose garden?"

"Yeah, anything you want babe. It's no problem."

In the driver's seat Ethan fired up the engine. His thoughts were on his victory, but he needed to find out what Denise had said. He considered his strategy. Asking about Denise first would make him look weak, but if he asked another question first, it would make his question about Denise seem careless.

"Why are you so quiet?" Rio asked, jolting him back.

"No reason," he lied.

She looked at him knowingly. "You know what Ethan?"

"What?"

"You're amazing! You have so many people who love you blindly. They listen to what you say without a second thought. You know how many people would give anything to have that type of power? That girl Denise is absolutely in love with you and she's so hurt, not because you're with me but because you have neglected her. She's got a plan to explain everything to everybody at school so that she can clear your name. If she does what she's planning on doing, I think you should kiss her."

Ethan took his eyes off the road as shock registered from what he just heard. "Excuse me?"

"You should kiss her," Rio repeated. "A kiss is the most wonderful thing two people can share. The great Shadow says, 'What does a kiss mean? Hello? Goodbye? Like a wedding or a wake? Or is it an expression of how you feel or how you want to feel? The acceptance of your kiss is just as good as you giving one.'"

Ethan shook his head. "What's wrong with you, Rio? You become my girlfriend, then you want me to kiss another girl? Quoting some homeless guy to validate it? Are you playing me? Why haven't I met your family?"

The shock written across her face was painfully apparent. He didn't let up.

"Well, are you going to explain? Are you going to tell me why you're so ashamed of me?"   Tears poured from her eyes. His words had an effect he hadn't intended. He had never seen her cry before.

"Stop the car," she screamed. "Stop the car!"

"Rio, wait honey. I'm sorry. I – I – I didn't mean…"

"No, you said what you thought. You don't speak your mind unless you believe it. I'm not ashamed of you. You're the best thing that's ever happened to me. What I'm ashamed of is that I was wrong; I'm not good enough for you."

"But Rio, wait! I – I…"

The car came to a stop because of a traffic light. Before the light could change colors, she was gone.

The next morning came to Ethan after a night of torment. Images of his mistakes danced through his mind until he woke to the weight of all he had lost. *'The reason you won't play football again is because you made the mistake. It's your fault. You screwed this up. No one else is to blame.'* Ethan's waking thought was that he might as well have plunged the blade into himself.

His father was home, and Ethan wished he wasn't. The once proud man tiptoed around like an indentured servant instead of the role model he'd once been. No more traveling for business trips, only nine to five in the city; a penance to Ethan's mother, not something he truly wanted to do. Mom appeared to be happy, but her happiness did not always seem genuine. How could she be truly happy? Her husband may be home, but he was not living as he wanted and was only home out of his obligation to them. Ethan felt trapped in this imaginary game of house where he played the role of the child. They were all characters playing the part of a family for an audience that wasn't there.

The reality of the moment hit him again, he'd pushed away the one person in this world who understood him. Foolishly he assumed he'd never met her family because she was too ashamed but in reality, he didn't know the reason.

"Honey?" His mom entered the room, "are you going to be back by dinner time?"

More make-believe family time, he thought. "Yeah Mom, I'll be here."

She came over and put her arms around him.

"If you want you can invite Rio."

The sound of pain into Ethan's ears. *Rio!*

"No Mom, Rio won't be able to come." Pain enveloped him, choking his ability to say anything more.

"Ethan, there will always be times in people's lives when they have to understand themselves so that they can understand other people. When two people love each other, they find a way to work through the rough parts in their differences. I guarantee whatever is troubling you kids will pass and you'll both learn something valuable."

"Thanks, Mom," he said kissing her on the cheek, glad the talk was over. All he wanted now was to hurry out of the make-believe happy-home, so he could see Rio.

When the lunch bell rang the entire school was talking about one topic. It was not unusual for everyone to be talking about him, but the reason today was different. Denise had written a front-page article on Ethan's contribution to their class in the school newspaper. She expressed how their class would be remembered throughout the school's history as one of the greatest because of his accomplishments. It was a touching and profound article, whose author made it all the more noteworthy. The only problem was that Rio wasn't there to share in this victory. She had not come to school. Her absence left him dizzy and looking for answers. People spoke to him and he had to search for the words to speak back. He walked on autopilot, not remembering how he'd gotten where he was. Everything seemed a blur. All he could think about was her.

"Hi, Ethan," said a familiar sweet voice. Denise. "Did you see the article I wrote in the paper?"

He stared at her, remembering each occasion he'd touched her body and how she always cried out in ecstasy. He did make her feel good. He leaned in and kissed her passionately, but he was thinking only of his love. It wasn't her mouth. It wasn't the taste he wanted. He pulled away feeling tainted and disgusted. What had he done? Rio told him to. His love told him to do this? Why did she tell him it would feel good? He couldn't take it. He rushed past the confused girl toward his trusty white horse, determined to confess to his thoughts to his love.

Ethan drove recklessly through the streets, still on autopilot, debating whether to go to Rio's house or not. He wondered why she'd been wrong about kissing Denise. His mind raced with unanswered possibilities. His demons returned. *Everything you do gets messed up! Look at your family! Wanna play football, stupid?* For hours he drove in circles contemplating his destination, stopping several times in different places attempting to rationalize the situation. Finally, he made the decision.

It was night when Ethan reached Rio's house. Darkness covered it so well that the home looked as if the lit windows floated in mid-air. The air was cold on his skin as he walked up the driveway, his breath hung heavy in the frigid air. He felt a kind of nervousness he'd never felt before, anxious and excited. He only wanted to show her that she had nothing to be ashamed of.

Ethan saw through the window before he could knock on the door, tears streaming down Rio's cheeks. His stomach dropped, and his heart began to pound in his chest as if trying to escape. Unable to catch his breath, Ethan closed his eyes to take away the scene, but it was now etched in his mind. The reason she hadn't taken him to her home was why she was so ashamed. Her stepfather was on top of her, pounding away at her innocence. In a split-second Ethan knew what he had to do. He beat at the door. He kicked the door. The door came down.

The flashing lights blanketed the sky stealing the darkness that had so recently covered the house. Ethan looked out through the window of a police patrol car. His clothes were soaked in blood. A teary-eyed Rio stood talking to officers. When they were done she mouth the words '*thank you*' and smiled meekly as the patrol car pulled off.

"What made you do that to your friend's stepfather, son?" The man in the suit asked from the front passenger seat. "Why would you attack a good man, a Reverend who's done nothing but good for our community?"

Ethan just stared at the detective for a moment. The suited man must be stupid, he thought. Why else would he ask such a question?

"Do you hear me, kid?" The detective asked.

"Yeah, I hear you."

"Well, why did you do that to the Reverend?"

Ethan remained silent, wondering again if the man could really be so stupid. Or did he have another agenda?

"Didn't she tell you what happened?" Ethan said with an attitude.

The detective laughed. "What she told us kid, will put you away for the rest of your life. You may want to come up with your own side of the story."

Confused, Ethan blurted out, "do you know what he was doing to her?"

"Yeah," the detective says with his own attitude, "he was teaching his step-daughter the Bible as he always does after dinner. He's probably gonna die, kid. You messed him up pretty bad."

"What? What the hell are you talking about?"

"We know she didn't do it. That's her story, what's yours? I'm giving you the chance to come up with an explanation that might help you get some treatment or help, because you're in a lot of trouble kid."

Ethan couldn't believe what he was hearing. Rio didn't say that. She couldn't have said that. It had to be a trick. "I want a lawyer,"

"You're gonna get one kid. Lawyers seem to flock to cases like this, but it really doesn't matter here because you were caught red-handed with an eye witness. The best thing you could look forward to is maybe getting out before you're an old man."

Ethan sat in a little room with a table and two-way mirror trying to figure out what happened. That is why she told him to kiss Denise. She wanted him to understand how it felt to have unwanted physical contact. Every night her stepfather must have raped her; torturing her with her own body. Even though she lied, he felt good that he had rescued her. At least she would not have to be ashamed anymore.

The cops processed him for hours before walking him down a long hallway. This day was almost over. Ethan was physically and emotionally exhausted when he reached the door to the cell. He walked in, feeling a sense of relief as the hard steel door closed behind him. The man on the bed turned over and smiled. It was Jake.

The next morning Denise typed in a daze. She was the first to find out. She'd been at Ethan's house when his family got the news. She had been waiting there to confess her love to him. That kiss… That passionate kiss. Blinded by tears, she typed the front page for the next school paper. The headline read: *Remember His Glory: Goodbye to the King.*

Part Three
Curse of The Fantasy Reflection

She sat in her favorite seat, an old rocking chair she had picked
up many years before, listening to its motion break the silence in her
home. She found its song soothing, in a place filled with long periods
of quiet. No television, no radio, no computer. Forbidden things.
Many things had been forbidden.

The telephone echoed over the chair's song.

"Hello," she answered calmly.

"Mom," the caller replied.

"Rio, is that you?"

"Yeah, Mom, it's me."

"Good. Good," she said, "this means you've seen your sister and
your father?"

"Yes, Mom, I've seen them both."

"Then I should be seeing you soon?"

"Yes, Mom, I'll be home soon."

"We have a lot to do. Please hurry. I miss you."

"I miss you too, Mom. I love you."

"I love you too. See you soon."

Night descended as she happily rocked in her favorite chair. She'd
spent many dark nights in this place, but this night was different. This
night offered her light. The burdens placed on her life faded into this
night. She found herself no longer trapped by the fear of *what if,* a
terror that had plagued her for so long she almost knew nothing else.
She was only a child when happiness went away. Drained of love and
joy, she lived with misery and misery's favorite companions; stress
and sadness. Her dreams had been taken, exchanged for a
hopelessness that lived in lonely isolation, for a reason she did not
understand.

Waiting for Rio to return, she said a prayer for Eva, thankful that
Eva was now in a better place, no longer in pain; her oldest daughter
can rest now. Her relief pooled in her eyes, washing over her vision,

her mind drifted to back to when all these dark nights began.

Since Shannon could remember, home had always been a place she hated. Her parents were alcoholics who spent most of their time lost in their own world, making brief appearances to sling nasty words at their only child. The little girl was forced into adulthood prematurely, her survival depended on her own ability to feed and clothe herself; rarely did she have parental supervision, rarely did they ask how she was or where she was going. Soon, she too was drinking, slowly turning into the very thing she despised. Little did she know, something was coming to alter everything in her life.

One day, while cutting school, Shannon walked alone in a park near her home. She came across a horribly disfigured man. His appearance was hard on her eyes and brought up thoughts she didn't want to acknowledge. The desolate park held no one else for her distraction. Shannon moved past the man, feeling sorry for him thankful she wasn't disfigured that way.

"You want to hear a joke?" The man's deep, scratchy voice pulsed through her chest. Shannon kept moving, pretending not to hear him. "It's a pretty funny joke. It would be a shame for you not to hear it."

Against her better judgment she stopped and turned to him, avoiding his face. "Excuse me?" She said as if she had not heard him clearly.

"Do you want to hear a joke or not?" The man snapped back.

Her gaze ventured from his chest to his face and found herself wondering what happened to deform him in such a way. It looked as if he'd been burnt, but not by a fire, maybe by some type of chemical. Whatever it was, the thought of it made Shannon cringe.

"It's not polite to stare, young lady! Didn't your parents teach you any manners? What's your name?"

"My – my name is Shannon."

"Well, Shannon, my name is Chris and I'm going to tell you a joke: What always gets lost, never gets found, is always searched for, but has been right there the whole time?"

She looked at the man curiously wanting to know the answer, "I don't know."

"The truth! The truth is always lost, never found, always searched for and been right there the whole time. Why is a young girl like you walking through a park in the middle of a school day all by herself, drinking? Don't you have any friends?"

"Your joke was cool, but we're not. I don't have to explain anything to you. So, if you don't mind, I'll be going on about my day."

Turning to walk off she expected him to say something, but his silence was more awkward than anything he could have said. After she'd taken a few steps she again felt his voice resonate in her chest. "The pain you feel only becomes worse when you refuse to accept it. Listen to yourself. I did not cause your anger, I simply reminded you it was here."

She continued walking but the man's words echoed in her mind. Much of her night was spent thinking about their encounter. The man's horrible face danced around her recollections. She felt her body convulse as she tried to ignore what was calling her attention. After some time, she relinquished her resistance and began to find beauty in his flaws. He was right; he had not caused her anger. He had only brought it to her attention.

Outside into the night she walked cold and alone with no specific destination to go, wondering how to escape. Tears poured from this old wound as she searched the dark for the truth to heal this place of suffering.

"You looking for somebody?" A voice called from behind.

Startled, scared, and in need of a drink, she turned to see her future. A woman just like her, only older and with a healthy, happy face full of peace and love. "Um, no I'm not looking for anyone. I'm just passing through."

"It's kind of late to be passing through. This neighborhood can be dangerous at night. Are you sure you're alright?"

The small gesture of kindness was something Shannon hadn't felt in a long time. The sincerity in the woman's voice and eyes was so overwhelming that Shannon couldn't hold back her tears when she tried to answer. The woman moved slowly with her arms open to embrace her. When she reached her, the woman wrapped Shannon in the warmth of security, melting more tears from the young girl's eyes.

"It's gonna be all right sweetheart. You're safe now. Everything is going to be alright."

Shannon went to the woman's house and, for the first time in years, ate a dinner that she did not have to prepare herself. Shannon felt wrapped in a cloud, wearing warm pajamas under a soft blanket. The woman tucked Shannon into a comfy bed before asking her if she needed anything else. Looking deep into the woman's eyes, Shannon saw so much love she couldn't help but smile, the first time in years she has done so without the aid of alcohol. The woman leaned in and kissed her gently on the forehead.

"I'm glad to see your spirit is happy. You have a good night's sleep and we'll talk in the morning. If you need anything, I'm right down the hall. Good night."

"Good night."

After the woman left, Shannon laid awake for a while, afraid to go to sleep for fear it was all a dream. Then it struck her, something she'd forgotten. Out of bed, Shannon quietly crept down the hallway to the woman's room. It was dark, and the house was quiet. Every step seemed to creak on the wood floor. At the opening to the woman's room Shannon knocked and stood frozen in the doorway. The woman turned to look.

"Is everything all, right?" The woman asked.

Shannon stood there, embarrassed. "Um – um I forgot to, um tell you. My name is Shannon."

"That's a beautiful name," the woman said, "my name is Claudia."

The morning came quickly, and Claudia woke Shannon with breakfast. The smell was delightful to her senses. A feeling of warmth embraced her as if she was home.

While eating breakfast, Shannon's smile grew larger and deeper. She found herself giggling here and there with absolute joy. She could barely contain herself from jumping up and down with laughter. Claudia smiled at the joy Shannon expressed.

"I see your spirit is happy," Claudia said. "Is there anything you would like to talk about? I will help you with whatever I can."

Shannon's smile faded as reality snuck back into her head; her parents, her school, and her life started to blind her with tears. Claudia's gentle arms wrapped around her.

"Stay present in this moment. Right now, you are away from what's hurting. You are in a safe place to face it. Be present. What are you running from?"

In the moment Shannon realized she wasn't with her parents, her school, or her loneliness; she was safe, and it was time for her to heal. Time for her to talk through the tears and pain. To find the truth's presence.

"The place I come from is full of pain. Last night I finally left that place and found you. I'm so afraid that this is only a dream, and that soon I will wake to find myself back in the place I left before we met. I'm scared, Claudia! I'm scared!"

"Shhh…" Claudia soothed Shannon while stroking her hair. "There's nothing to fear here. I will not leave you and I will not send you back to the place you came from. You are welcome to stay here as long as you like. Please consider this your home."

The tears pouring from Shannon's eyes, began to change. Instead of heavy sadness, they were filled with joy. Her pain drifted away, and with each cry her wounds were cleansed by tears of salvation. She was free.

Months of good times followed that day. Shannon's new home was a place of comfort and joy. Seeing Claudia's face and hearing her words was something Shannon always looked forward to. Shannon had no desire to leave, no reason for stress; everything she needed or wanted was with her. Most mornings were spent gardening in the backyard, tending to the flowers, fruits, and vegetables. Claudia taught her how to make dishes from clay and weave her own clothes. Shannon learned how to truly live in this world, not just survive.

Shannon and Claudia's life became a beautiful routine until one evening when Claudia disappeared. Shannon was terrified that Claudia had abandoned her. All her fears of the past flooded the moment. As dawn approached, Claudia crept through the door; a crown of flowers upon her head. Shannon, eyes red and puffy, inquired, "Where have you been?"

Claudia smiled and said, "I have been traveling in the light of darkness."

Shannon stopped crying and with a puzzled expression asked, "What does that mean?"

Claudia smiled again and said, "One day you will know. It's time for bed."

The disappearances continued without further word or question, until one especially odd day.

Shannon was working in the garden, tending to the flowers like normal, when Claudia came out holding one of the flower crowns she always returned home with after her travels in the light of darkness. She set the crown down next to Shannon.

"I want you to make some of these," she said while picking fresh flowers from the garden.

"Ok, just show me how," Shannon replied innocently.

Claudia knelt down with the flowers and began to weave the flowers together; soon they reveal themselves to be a beautiful garland. Shannon watched intently, studying how to make the flower ring. When Claudia was done she placed the finished crown on Shannon's head. The young girl repeated what she'd seen, and before long she'd made a dozen rings. Claudia called her into the house for dinner. Shannon rose from the ground, as if possessed by a great spirit, and began to dance, imagining she was a princess in a ballroom. Even after eating dinner with Claudia she twirled and danced for her audience, the flowered crown still atop her head until she was claimed by sleep.

"Wake up, young Shannon," Claudia's soft whisper beckoned. "Wake up. It's time for you to travel in the light of darkness."

The moon and the stars lit the night sky above her. How did she get outside? She looked around to see that they were in a forest surrounded by people dressed as trolls and fairies, all wearing flowered garlands on their heads. Too afraid to say a word, Shannon lay speechless. Claudia smiled.

"There is nothing to fear here, young Shannon. We are all friends. Just as I care for you, they also care. Just as you were lost, and I found you. I was once lost, and they found me. You were brought to us, young Shannon by a force that even I cannot explain with words. Isn't that right, Chris?"

Shannon looked to see the horribly burned man from the park, whose words drove Shannon to leave her old home. How could this man be standing next to Claudia? He was speaking but Shannon couldn't comprehend the words. Her attention had been captured by a looming shadow.

A man emerged from the darkness. His face emanated peace and wisdom; his eyes soothed Shannon's uneasy emotions.

"Hello, Shannon. My name is Shadow, and I travel behind the light in search of lost souls. We've all been eagerly waiting to meet you and bask in the beauty you radiate. Tonight, we mark and celebrate your oneness. Do not be afraid. We are all just as you are and once just as you were. The flowers you've grown in the garden drape our heads. The rings you made have been given to certain people among us."

Shannon looked around. "Yes, you're wearing one of the rings I made and so is Chris."

"Let us celebrate!" Chris shouted.

The crowd of costume creatures erupted in cheers.

"Come, allow me to take your hand." Shadow said extending an open palm.

Shannon reached to accept his invitation. They walked toward a circle of stones through soft grass, which gently folded beneath their feet. Every step for Shannon became a different experience of the moment. A future she saw getting closer. Her guide released her hand to seize the power of her choices. Shannon stood in the center of the stones with Shadow while the others lined its perimeter.

"Can you feel the energy of the moon?" Shadow enquired, backing away from her, "look at the moon, young Shannon. Look at the moon and feel its power."

Looking at the bright blue moon she became lost in its beauty. It seemed to grow and move closer. It is alive! Moving in a circle, drawing her energy, absorbing her weight until her feet no longer touched the ground; the soft blades of grass no longer beneath her.

"Feel free, young Shannon. Travel the light of darkness. See yourself as a formless being created by this universe to travel its moments of space and time. You have no origin or final destination. You have always been and always will be. This form you possess is merely a phase in your existence. Feel your inner and outer connection to the universe. The spirit of creation is inside you and all around you."

The force that lifted her from the ground took her away from form. A soothing, melodic hum lulled her.

Shannon woke with the morning sun, the crown of flowers still atop her head. She was in the same place she had danced herself to sleep the night before. *Was it all a dream?* She had to know if it was real.

"Claudia! Claudia," Shannon yelled out, running to the older woman's room. "I had this wonderful dream that we traveled the light of darkness and I met all of your friends to celebrate my healing."

Claudia said nothing. She didn't even acknowledge Shannon's presence in the doorway. She just stared at her reflection as she stood in front of the mirror, as if nothing else existed.

"Claudia! Claudia, is everything ok?" Shannon asked with concern.

"I'm fine," Claudia said without turning to look at her. "Please leave. I'll be out in a moment."

"Okay Claudia, I want to tell you about this dream I had."

"It wasn't a dream. Please close the door behind you."

Shannon closed the door, reminded of her old life. At least it wasn't a dream.

Claudia emerged a few minutes later and began making breakfast. Shannon watched her from outside in the garden feeling better knowing Claudia cares about her. She had burst into her room without even saying hello or good morning. Who responds well to something like that? She put down the gardening tools and returned to the house.

Claudia was humming and singing while making breakfast. "Good morning, Shannon! Hurry and get washed up. Breakfast is ready."

After quickly washing up Shannon returned and Claudia waiting for her with a smile.

"Did you enjoy yourself last night?" Claudia asked.

"Yes! Yes, I enjoyed myself a great deal. At first I was afraid because I didn't know how we got there but as time went on I truly felt at peace and nothing else mattered."

"Yes, I was afraid too, the first time I met the great Shadow at the Circle of the Moon. I came to the light of darkness the same way as you."

"You did?"

Claudia laughed at the young girl's innocence. "You have a very beautiful spirit young Shannon. The first of our group to be with the great Shadow was Chris. He and Shadow have been together for many moons. The next to join was my teacher, Crystal."

"Was she there last night?"

"No, young Shannon. Her consciousness passed from that form many years ago. Many years of suffering and abuse before meeting the great Shadow claimed that life."

"Oh, I'm – I'm sorry to hear that."

"Do not be sorry young Shannon. Her existence was at peace before she left this world, and that's what's important."

"I wish I could have met her."

"You have already met her through the energy and teachings she has passed to you through me. Let us finish breakfast so that we can start preparing for the next moon."

"All right!"

They ate for a moment in silence. Then, "Claudia?"

"Yes, young Shannon?"

"I'm – I'm sorry for coming into your room like that this morning. Please forgive me."

"All is forgiven young Shannon. Eat your food."

The next moon arrived, and Shannon was ready with plenty of flower rings and plenty of rest behind her. Not wanting to miss anything she sat in the dark, waiting with a smile on her face.

Tap, tap on the windowpane. *Tap, tap* on the windowpane again.

Claudia rushed in from her bedroom. "We must go, young Shannon. The light of the darkness awaits us."

Shannon looked around to see if she could find who had tapped on the window as they left into the night. They made their way through the dense forest to a clearing where the others were gathered. Everyone sat silently, still and frozen. Claudia put her finger to her lips gesturing to stay quiet and then pointed to an area for them to sit down. Shannon smiled with delight, occasionally catching the eyes of others who smiled back at her. Shadow and Chris appeared from the forest. They walked around, greeting each in attendance with focused silence. Once they had traveled to every person, Chris raised his hand and, speaking in a whisper, he began.

"Why do we have to be so quiet, Claudia?"

"So as to be aware of any attention we may have drawn to our travels."

"Is it bad if a stranger discovers us?"

A brief pause as Claudia considered the question.

"I can't say whether it would be bad or good. What I can say is our meetings are very private, and no one should take that for granted. The great Shadow is getting ready to speak."

The wise man with peace in his eyes stood proud as everyone gathered around him.

"What some call God and the Devil, good and evil, we call life. The cycle of life is a constant struggle between counterparts. These opposing forces move existence and at the same time create diversity. We see this clearly throughout existence. Whenever we are pulled to one side, the other furiously attempts to pull us back. That is why we are here. Who will be our next seeker?"

Looking around Shannon noticed that everyone's hands were raised high in the air.

"I see we have a volunteer. Young Shannon, please stand and step forward."

She stepped forward embarrassed to be brought to the center, wondering what a 'seeker' was.

"Shannon, we look forward to seeing what you have to give. Chris, please explain to young Shannon what her duties will be."

"Come this way, our young seeker." Chris said.

Slowly she walked toward him as the rest of the group looked on.

As he sat down on a tree stump he said, "Your duties are not very difficult, the most important thing to learn is to spot. You must learn how to spot who can potentially be rescued from the clutches of a slanted perspective. Some people live in their own personal nightmare and simply don't know how to wake up; some don't even know they're asleep. Those are the ones you look for. You don't want to grab someone who knows the nightmare and enjoys it because they can pull you away from your perspective. It is very important to choose wisely. Do you understand?"

Hearing the duties Shannon found herself excited, but there was one thing she had to know. "Um, Chris. I understand the duties, and I see the importance of this work, but I don't understand why I've been chosen to do this."

The disfigured man laughed thinking of how many times he'd heard this. "Oh, young Shannon, just by making that statement you're going to do fine. We all became seekers after our first moon of healing. You are one of us."

His words did little to reassure her. She breathed a sigh of reluctance and gently embraced him.

"Oh yes, young Shannon. You are one of us!"

The next day Shannon was working in the garden as usual when Claudia came out.

"Shannon! You're not supposed to be here right now."

The young girl looked up with fresh earth for seedlings in her hands. "What do you mean, Claudia?"

"You're supposed to be seeking! You must get ready and leave at once. You may have already missed someone."

Feeling the urgency Shannon jumped up and hurried to get dressed. Within moments she was ready for the world. Claudia's bedroom door was closed when she came out. Shannon tried the knob, but it was locked.

"Claudia?" She called, lightly knocking on the door.

Silence.

"Claudia?" She said again, not sure if she spoke loud enough the first time.

Still, silence.

"Claudia?" She said even louder, knocking harder on the door.

"Shannon!" Claudia yelled, "please go. You should be seeking right now."

"I'm – I'm sorry Claudia. I just wanted to say goodbye."

Silence.

Shannon left feeling she had done wrong, and for the first time since meeting Claudia, Shannon entered the world without her. Drifting away from the neighborhood, she tried to focus on seeking but everyone she saw seemed to be a candidate. The business woman and her troubles, the homeless man and his troubles, everyone on the street seemed to be lost.

Shannon returned home at night feeling worse than when she left. Opening the unlocked door to their home she found a smiling, singing Claudia preparing dinner.

"How was your adventure?" The older woman asked warmly.

Claudia's effervescent energy caught Shannon off guard.

"Oh, young Shannon, your spirit has been injured. What happened?"

Shannon had been on the verge of tears before Claudia had said a word. One look at the woman brought Shannon to her breaking point.

"Claudia! I let you all down. I couldn't find anyone. Everybody looked the same. I'm not ready. I... I'm sorry. I'm so sorry."

"Shh, young Shannon, do not cry. You have done nothing wrong. In fact, you have done exactly as you were supposed to do."

"What do you mean? I don't understand."

Claudia smiled at the young, innocent life before her. Reminded that she once saw the world the same way.

"Let us sit, young Shannon."

The two women sad down in the cozy living room of the small two-bedroom home. The cushions of the sofa embraced them as they settled in. A small tea pot sat on the coffee table with two tea cups on either side as if it was known that this moment awaited them. Claudia poured the steaming water into the cups, dropping tea bags in each.

"Do you want a little honey in your tea?"

"Yes please," Shannon replied, taking off her shoes, wrapping a warm blanket around her feet as she snuggled deeper into the couch.

Claudia stirred honey into the tea and then handed the warm cup to Shannon.

"It's a mixture of herbs from the garden; it tastes like fruit."

Shannon took small sips and said, "Yeah, it's like a mix of strawberries and cherries, in warm water and honey."

They both laughed, enjoying the moment, not missing their pasts.

Claudia, still holding her smile, moved hair from in front of Shannon's eyes, stroking it back into place atop her head.

"When I was young I got involved with some people who were absolutely no good. They preyed on others whenever they had the chance. It had nothing to do with money, they wanted to make people pay for the way they felt."

Claudia's eyes glazed over, as her memory took her deep into her story.

"One day, walking downtown among the tall buildings and people I despise, I looked for someone to feel my pain. I spotted the perfect individual. A guy in a suit who looked like he could use some easy company, but what I had for him would be far from easy. After a few moments of sweet talking I had him all set to go to a hotel room when this lady bumped into us, dropping a bag of groceries. I looked at her with pure irritation, ready to pounce as she picked up her stuff which was everywhere. She didn't even say 'excuse me'. The guy in the suit began helping her pick up her things. The lady looked up at me and smiled; it was a smile which lives with me to this day. It was the most beautiful thing I had ever seen. Still looking at me a she said, 'A beauty like yours can only come from good things. Can you please help me?'

"I began to help her gather her things. Picking up the last items, she touched my hand and asked me to walk with her to the bus stop, stressing it would only take a minute. The guy in the suit agreed to wait while the lady and I walk to the bus stop. We moved in silence and when we got there the lady thanked me. I tell her it's no problem and turn to walk back towards the man in the suit. As I do so she said, 'I meant that about your beauty. You should treasure yourself and guard that treasure at all costs.'

"I continued to walk away from her. I didn't turn around for fear of the tears that would fall if I did. I had to complete my objective and go with the man in the suit."

A tear rolled down Claudia's cheek. Shannon sat her tea down and wrapped her arms around Claudia, consoling her as she continued.

"When the man and I reached the motel all I could hear was the woman's words echoing in my mind. At that moment, it hit me; if I go in the room with him, I will not be treasuring myself as a person. I told him I had to go check on something I left the motel. I was only a few blocks from the motel when I heard a voice from behind me say, 'It's time for you to come home child and enjoy the beauty of who you are.'

"That day was the beginning of my healing. That was the day I met Crystal of the night. She was the lady downtown who saved me.

"You see, young Shannon, seeking is not about knowing the other person, it's about knowing yourself. Remember how you were found and you will know how to find someone else the same way. It's not about looking for someone to save, it's about finding yourself. You'll know exactly what I mean when the time comes. It might take you two hours or two years, but when it happens you'll know what to do. Now, let's eat a little so that we can be well rested for the morning. Come."

Taking Shannon by the hand the two walked to the dinner table. Shannon was quiet as she ate, absorbing Claudia's story. She saw her in a new light as a real person, not a mythical Angel on a grandiose pedestal. That's what the story meant, they were one and the same.

"Claudia?"

"Yes, Shannon?"

"Who is it that taps on the window?"   Claudia laughed.

"Young Shannon, that's why I love your spirit so much... The tapper on the window is not a mystery once you find what you're seeking."

Claudia laughed at the young girl's face twisted in confusion.

"Young Shannon, always remember that there are no secrets in life, only answers to questions that we have not yet asked. You are going to make an excellent seeker. Be sure and get plenty of rest tonight. Seeking can be exhausting work."

Shannon woke before the sun, eager to begin seeking. The vigor of life flowed strongly though her veins. The streets were quiet as the rising sun brought light back to this portion of the world. Shannon reflected on her conversation with Claudia. She was in search of herself, looking for a reflection of who she once was in the face of another. Sitting in a park, Shannon watched people pass. Everyone seemed to have an important place to go. As she watched patiently, she noticed a boy walking aimlessly through the park. He seemed so familiar to her; Shannon realized she was watching her own reflections in him. The boy sat down at a bench shrouded in trees and took a drink from a bottle wrapped in a paper bag. She was eager to approach him but chose to continue watching.

The boy finished his drink and staggered from his spot underneath the trees. Clearly intoxicated, he moved where the wind took him. Shannon followed him out of the park, two strangers traveling the same path. Shannon knew it well. They were headed to a pool hall-pizza parlor frequented by lots of other teenagers. They boy walked up to a group of young men where he slapped high-fives and gave handshakes to greet them. After a few moments of laughing and talking they broke up to various tables and started hustling newcomers to the pool hall. Shannon chose a corner of the room where she wouldn't be noticed to watch him conduct his business. They boy was good at his hustle and he managed to continue successfully for hours. When he finally called an end to his day, Shannon instinctively knew why, it wasn't that he couldn't have continued at the pool hall, he needed a drink. He shook hands with a few of his buddies as he said hurried goodbyes while heading to the door. After waiting a few moments, she followed. The boy had not gone too far; she spotted him leaning against the wall on the side of a liquor store. Shannon kept her distance while she watched him make his move on a passing homeless man who needed the money worse than the boy needed a drink. A match made in hell, she thought. The homeless man took the deal and Shannon made her move.

"Why does the moon circle the Earth?" She asked, confident she was within earshot.

The boy looked at her squinting to see the features of the silhouetted form approaching him. "What?"

"Why does the moon circle the Earth?" Shannon repeated, louder and with greater confidence.

"I don't know, why?" He replied with annoyance as he took a drag of his cigarette.

"Think about the experience of our individual paths and the effects those routes make around us. The moon's path is to follow the Earth. What is yours?"

Thinking she must be crazy, the boy turned slowly and walked away. As if on cue the homeless man exited the store and the boy followed him to complete their transaction. As they crossed the street, Shannon called after him, "You can walk away from me, but every moment you're answering the question for yourself." The boy disappeared around a corner with the homeless man without giving Shannon another look.

Shannon walked, marking every step back to the park where she first laid eyes on him, sitting on the same bench, she waited. Every second seemed to pass as hours. Her mind was consumed with one question: *What if? What if the boy is her mirror and she his reflection?*

"Aye! Moon Girl," a voice shouted from behind, "if you wanted to hang out all you had to do is ask."

It was the boy.

"Okay," she said, "let's hang out."

He smiled at her unemotional response.

"You have a name, Moon Girl?"

Shannon didn't respond.

"Alright, Moon Girl, my name is Charles. You wanna hang out, huh? Then come on." He walked a few steps, but Shannon stood still.

"I thought you wanted to hang, Moon Girl. What's up?"

Staring into his eyes, she could see he was up to no good. "Charles, do you know the difference between 'yes' and 'no'?"

"No," he said, "I don't know what the difference is."

She smiled.

"Yes, you do. Imagine if you'd have answered, *yes* instead of *no*; you'd have gotten a different response."

"So, I guess that's the answer to your riddle?"

"You're very smart, Charles. Now we can hang out. Come with me."

They made their way to a spot Shannon had enjoyed in the past. High atop a hill covered by tall trees and thick bush, a thin, unmarked trail led the way to their hidden destination.

"Wow, Moon Girl, you can see over the entire park from here. I've climbed this hill a thousand times and have never seen this place."

Shannon was busy breaking overgrown branches, revealing a small wooden bench.

"You can have a seat here if you'd like," she said.

"Yeah, thanks, Moon Girl. You still haven't told me how you know about this place and why I've never seen you before."

"You're funny, Charles. Why should I know you and why should you know this place? Why ask me a question that works just as good when you ask yourself the same thing?"

"Moon Girl, what are you talking about?"

"I'm talking about your mind, Charles. The world does not revolve around you. I don't know you for the same reason you don't know me, and this place is new to you because you've never been here." "Damn, Moon Girl, I was just trying to ask a question. I didn't mean to offend you."

"I'm not offended. I built this place a long time ago. I used to come here to escape the world around me. Here, I could be alone and watch the world from a distance. I could see people without them seeing me. They couldn't judge me. They couldn't control me. Here, I was free."

"That sounds pretty lonely, Moon Girl. You didn't have many friends, huh?"

"Friends were not what I needed, because I was not alone. I had something with me that I treasured more than any person, including myself. I had something that gave me more comfort than a vanishing friend ever could; my drink. It didn't matter what kind it was as long as it was strong and worked fast.

"You see that spot over there? I dug a deep hole in the middle of those bushes, so I could throw up when I got too drunk. A true alcoholic, as I learned from the best. That's why, when I saw you, I knew."

"Aw, Moon Girl, you got me all wrong. I love to drink, but I don't do it like that! I party with my buds and we drink a little. I might get a little wasted before and after I go meet them but that's the only time I drink alone. I'm a social drinker who loves to hang out. I'm sorry your trip was so bad but mine's alright."

"Yours is alright? Your trip is alright? Trips like yours create trips like mine. My parents were social drinkers until the social ran out. They met partying and never stopped. I was born addicted to alcohol. When I took my first drink, I was already hooked. So, when you say your trip isn't that bad, you think about the future you're creating. You could have a little girl just like me. Wouldn't that be nice?" Silence. She continued, "If you love yourself, you'll heed my words. If not, enjoy the child you create from madness. I'll see you tomorrow." She moved toward the thick bushes and tall trees.

Charles sat quiet absorbing her words before blurting out, "Moon Girl! How will I know when and where to meet you?"

She stopped but didn't turn around. "You will know the same way I will. We'll just see each other Charles." Vanishing into the bushes and trees, she left him with his thoughts.

It was evening when Shannon walked through the door. The delicious smell of dinner permeated the house. The table was set for two.

"Claudia," she called, "Claudia! I'm home and I have good news."

"That's wonderful," Claudia shouts from the bedroom. "Get washed up and we'll talk about it over dinner."

Shannon quickly washed up thinking how much she had to say. Claudia sat at the dinner table, smiling. "Have a seat, young Shannon. I'm sure during your travels you neglected to eat; that usually happens during seeking."

At that moment Shannon realized Claudia was right, she hadn't eaten anything all day. From the first bite, she was consumed by the flavors, as if discovering a new delicacy. As the taste washed over Shannon's tongue, Claudia's melodic voice wafted to her ears.

"On my first mission into the world, I became lost and it took me a long time to find my way home; I became removed by what I was seeking. You see young Shannon, finding your reflection brings you closer to yourself. During the search, you will discover new things that have always been. You will recall moments that feel as if they were dreams. You will begin to see yourself. Once you fully see yourself, you will finally be free. Your journey today is only a small glimpse of this mirror. You still have so much to see. It is time that you rest, young Shannon. Tomorrow will bring about a new journey. It is your time, spend it wisely."

Shannon took the last bites of her meal, chewing in a daze, too tired to respond. Drawn to her bedroom, before her head hit the pillow, she was fast asleep.

Shannon found Charles by the liquor store.

"Moon Girl," he called out smiling. "I'm glad to see you. I

thought a lot about what you said. Today is going to be my last day drinking. I want to hang with you, but I don't want to remind you of things you went through."

"Charles, you don't have to worry about me. We'll do what you want to do."

"I really don't want too much, Moon Girl. All I want to do is hang at that spot with you and talk."

"That sounds cool, Charles. We can go there. Come on."

They traveled to the hill top where they sat on the bench watching the people below do what people do. They sat in silence. Charles continued to drink, saying farewell to his good friend. He leaned over and kissed Shannon gently on the lips. It was a passionate kiss that Shannon found herself unexpectedly enjoying. She felt the urge to pull away but didn't. Shannon opened her eyes, still in her bed at Claudia's. That kiss, her time with Charles — it was all just a dream? It was still dark outside. Remembering she hadn't told Claudia about Charles, she crawled out of bed and walked to Claudia's room. Claudia wasn't there; the bed was made the room was cold.

"Claudia?" Shannon called out, walking into the room, "Claudia?" She called again, with still no response. She turned on a lamp by the bed and saw something move out of the corner of her eye. She turned to see horrifying, hideous images in the mirror. The mirror appeared fractured, each sliver showed a different version of her own reflection. In one she is young, in another, old; the next, perfect beauty, though in others every blemish, every mistake, every insecurity projected. Her heart was gripped by fear as her eyes grappled with the images before her, desperately trying to find which image in the shattered mirror belonged to her. The largest sliver showed her smiling and laughing with great joy, but in reality, her screams caused the slivers to split into more separate pieces. The image of her enraged flew toward her as if leaping through the mirror and into the world. As if it were too much for even the mirror to contain, the mirror exploded into shards onto the floor.

"What have you done?" Claudia screamed as she walked into the room.

"I – I – I didn't do anything Claudia. I – I came in to talk to you and saw this mirror and then it just broke. I didn't do anything. I swear Claudia. I swear."

Claudia knelt, picking up the pieces of broken glass; visibly shaken by the loss of her mirror. "Get out." She said sternly, looking up at Shannon with a coldness the young girl had never seen before in Claudia's face. It resembled the same rage that broke the mirror. "GET OUT!" Claudia yelled as she walked toward Shannon with a piece of the broken mirror still in her hand. "Now! Shannon, I want you gone now!"

"Claudia? I didn't do anything wrong."

Claudia slapped Shannon viciously across the face. Tears streamed from Shannon's eyes. Claudia slapped her as her mother had done. In shock, Shannon ran from the bedroom, through the living room, out the door, down the street, and down another and another until she had no more breath left to run.

Life with Charles was good for a while. They had both given up alcohol. Shannon worked as a waitress in a sports bar owned by Charles' father. She thought it was funny that she, an ex-alcoholic with no desire to take a drink, worked at a bar. They had purchased a home of their own and were deeply in love, raising their one-year old daughter Eva. They attended church services every Sunday and genuinely seemed to be the perfect young family in the neighborhood.

Shannon left work early one day to surprise her husband and young daughter at home. Arriving at the house she noticed an unfamiliar car in the driveway. Charles always had friends and family dropping by, so the car didn't spark any concern. When opening the door, a smell entered Shannon's nose and her heartbeat skipped. It wasn't the smell that tripped up her heart; but the image before her that did it. Charles sat on the couch with a beautiful woman, playing with their daughter. It wasn't an alarming scene, but it was one Shannon would never forget. It marked the beginning of the end of their marriage. The smell of this woman's perfume lingered in Shannon's mind as the fragrance of anguish. Shadow had explained to Shannon in a dream that the curse of the broken mirror would see to it that Shannon would never be able to hold love from anyone, and if she ever attempted to love, that love would be taken from her.

Shannon was four months pregnant with their second child when Charles ran away with his mistress. Charles' father offered to help, but Shannon refused, knowing the curse she carried would only harm their relationship if she stayed. Instead, Shannon took refuge from her mounting pains and increasing pressures at the church. The Reverend became her counsel and she his aid. They worked closely together day and night. Shannon's belief in religion gave her comfort to face herself. Her God knew what was best and would take care of her. The Reverend was part of the Lord's plan. Through the Reverend the Lord delivered sermons; the Reverend's words were spoken from the heavens, each syllable stroked Shannon's spirit, ushering in a spirit of salvation.

Over time Shannon and the Reverend found love, triumphing over Shannon's fears; she trusted in the Lord's will. They hid their secret from the world as long as they could, but it was a love too strong to stay hidden. A Deacon at the church found out and assumed that the child Shannon was carrying belonged to the Reverend. The congregation called for them to leave the church.

The couple purchased a home on a few acres of land in a new town. On the edge of their property, the Reverend built a church out of an old barn and soon people in the small town were attending Sunday service there. All seemed to be well, but the Reverend had grown cold since being forced to leave his previous church. Shannon hoped that once the new church filled up with parishioners the Reverend's cold heart would melt, but it didn't. Instead his anger and hatred only grow. He forbade Shannon from leaving the property and bound Eva to the house. Whenever Eva ventured outside, he beat her savagely. Eventually, he'd had enough of her disobedience. He took Eva outside and didn't bring her back. Shannon begged the Reverend for her daughter, but he refused; saying Eva was possessed by the devil and he would have no part of the devil in his home. The loss of her first daughter tore deep into Shannon's heart; another part of her died. The curse of the broken mirror was the curse of a broken heart and Shannon paid dearly for it every day.

The Reverend found a different way to rob Shannon of her youngest daughter. The child that forced him from his beloved congregation would be his and his alone. The Reverend used a softer touch with Rio, praising her constantly, and keeping her all to himself. Shannon was not even allowed to touch her. Rio was raised to believe that the Reverend was her father, the only father she should ever know. He kept Rio and Shannon separated, discarding Shannon while coveting Rio. Rio slept in the Reverend's bed while Shannon was made to sleep in the basement. Only after the Reverend and Rio had eaten was Shannon allowed to come out and eat. Most of the day Shannon was forced to stay in her dark and cold part of the house away from Rio and the Reverend. She spent her time watching rats scurry across the floor and spiders spin their webs. The water heater was her only source of heat in the winter, warmth she shared with the rodents and insects. What had she done to deserve this?

Seeing her young daughter, her heart ached with despair. She wanted to love this young life, but fear of the curse that caged her heart. She watched her young daughter grow as a stranger. The child would call out "the lady," smiling and waving when she saw Shannon. One day Rio called out in front of the Reverend when she saw Shannon, "The lady! The lady!" causing the Reverend to beat Shannon in front of young Rio. From then on, Rio didn't call out when she saw Shannon, she simply smiled and waved.

Many nights Shannon cried herself to sleep as she begged the heavens for an end to this suffering. Without salvation she woke in despair, still in the nightmare. She searched her soul to find comfort, only to discover demons dwelling near her spirit. She struggled to find reasons to live; the curse meant she couldn't be with her children. The Reverend hated her. Even if she ran away the curse would surely follow. There was only one way out. She managed to steal pain pills from the medicine cabinet and poured herself a glass of wine. First the pills, then the wine. The taste of alcohol went down smooth, warming her chest as she swallowed, welcoming her old friend from so long ago. Why had she stopped in the first place? Her drinking in exchange for this? Had she not met Chris, had she not met Claudia, what would her life be? Certainly better off as an alcoholic than an animal locked in a prison of this nature. Cursed because she tried to do good. She laughed at being tortured by a Reverend. Of all the people to be harmed by! A Reverend had broken her spirit into pieces not possible for reconstruction. He had given her comfort, only to take it away. She laughed as tears trickled down her face. All this pain, all this hurt, all this loneliness because of a broken mirror. And that was the funniest thing of all – how had she broken the mirror? Was it her reflection? Or had the mirror been broken the entire time? If her reflection had broken the mirror, then the mirror was correct. She was hideous; her reflection was already cursed. If the mirror had broken some other way, it was a cruel twist of fate. Lying in her bed, the room began to spin. As the world spiraled into oblivion, Shannon reflected on her cruel fate: *Every time you encounter love, it is taken away.*

"Your vision is beyond the reflection of love." The deep, raspy voice bellowed from somewhere behind her. She turned over to see Shadow. "Young Shannon, the mirror only showed you the many ways of yourself. Each sliver being a piece of you."

"Shadow…" She whispered with her last bit of energy. "It's all your fault! Had I not met you... I wouldn't be here. I hate you... I wish I had never met you!" She turned away, closing her eyes to stop the tears.

The large Shadow looming above her knelt down to run his fingers through her hair. "We showed you a glimpse of yourself. You've always been traveling this path, this detour from love. There is always an opposite or a parallel to all forces in the universe. You run parallel to love. Instead of knowing love deeply, you have only known it though fleeting moments. Intersecting love's path by crossing it. You'll have no idea where the intersection is, but it is your journey to find it and feel when to stop.

"In order to enter the path of love, you must find your soulmate. This person will travel the same way as you, yet on a different path. You share an undefined relationship with this person because of your lack of interaction. In the beginning, the moments you share will be less than seconds, but the love you both reflect will be present in every encounter. When you find this person, it will be your duty to guide them. You will have to figure out where and how to consolidate your paths and break this curse. Once you have entered the path of love together, I will come for you and your soul mate. That is how you'll know you are free. Enjoy your sleep, young Shannon, it's almost time..."

"WAKE UP! WAKE UP SHANNON!" The Reverend yelled, roughly slapping her across the face. "You will not desecrate my home with your devilish sin. You're a heathen of life! Possessed by the devil!"

"What's wrong with the lady, Dad?" Little Rio asked sleepily from the darkened background.

"Nothing, child. Go grab a blanket and lay it on the seat in daddy's car."

He lifted Shannon from the bed, still cursing her for her foolishness. His words no longer carried the sting that once taunted her soul. His words no longer made her weak and confused, but now made her strong and able to understand the truth. Shadow had given her something to live for.

She laid on a blanket in the back seat of the car. The blanket was soft like the fur of new life cradling her; it comforted her more than anything had in years. Although she knew she was dying, she felt reborn and couldn't help laughing at the irony of her condition. She'd never felt more alive than she did now in death.

"Lady, are you okay?" Young Rio asked.

Shannon looked into the girl's eyes seeing something which used to frighten her, a sight which used to trouble her a great deal. She saw herself, but she was no longer ashamed of the reflection before her. For the first time in many years she was proud.

"Yes, young Rio, I'm fine."

"Rio what did I tell you about talking to the lady?"

Hearing the Reverend's voice Rio trembled and froze in place, still looking back at Shannon from the front passenger seat.

"What did I tell you, Rio?" The Reverend shouted.

Her voice was cautious and barely audible, "You told me not to speak to the lady. I'm sorry, Daddy. I'm sorry."

The tears that fell from Rio's eyes fell hard inside Shannon's heart. The callous Reverend was unmoved by tears and showed Rio no mercy. "You know I'm going to have to punish you for disobeying me."

"No Daddy! No, I – I didn't mean it. Please don't punish me. Please Daddy, please!"

Shannon could not stand to hear her daughter cry any longer. With her last bit of strength, she summoned a power from deep within. Though her voice had been weakened by death encroaching, she hissed her carefully chosen words with clarity and resolve, "Reverend if you harm her, your life will never find peace. *You leave my daughter alone.*"

The Reverend turned slowly toward her, fixing his eyes on the pitiful women dying in the back of his car. Paying no attention to the road he replied, "Are you threatening me, woman?"

"No Reverend, I'm warning you."

"I will not argue with a woman intoxicated to the point of flirting with death. Your warning means nothing to me and I will have no more words from you during the remainder of this drive. You understand me, woman?"

Shannon closed her eyes; her last words had exhausted her final remnants of strength. His power had been broken. This day marked the first of many that she would stand strong against the Reverend's dominance. That which is weak today can be strong tomorrow, for those on top face a constant battle. Shannon's first fight would be for the home, and then her daughter. The war began riding to the hospital. Through feeling the sinewy tendrils of death, she had tasted freedom and found her life's purpose.

Once home from the hospital, with clear determination, Shannon crossed every boundary the Reverend had set. She was expected to wait until he and Rio had eaten before she ate. One morning at sunrise Shannon walked into the kitchen and remained there until evening time; only leaving once to use the bathroom. The Reverend was furious and chastised her, but it has no effect. Now immune to his tactics, the next morning she did the same thing; and after only two days of this her point was made. The Reverend entered the kitchen on the third morning holding Rio's hand. He kept the child close as they ate their breakfast. Shannon knew that Rio was forbidden to speak to her. She did not expect Rio to even look at her, but as soon as the Reverend's face turned, Rio smiled and waved. Shannon smiled back with a warm heart; the spoils of war.

Shannon's next battle was to move from the basement into the guest room; this proved to be more difficult. Every time she moved her things, the Reverend moved them back to the basement. So, she decided to leave her things in the basement and sleep in the guest room without them. The Reverend removed the bed. Shannon slept on the floor. The Reverend removed the carpet and littered the floor with dirt. Shannon felt worse than she had in a long time. The guest room now looked as her previous dwelling had. This once prized room of the home lay in ruins because of her touch; a reminder of the curse. Still she could not give up. She ventured outside the house searching for peace, crossing another of the Reverend's boundaries. The flowers, the trees, the sky, and the sun all brightened her perspective. They seemed to celebrate her life with every step she took, giving her encouragement to continue. This is what she was fighting for. The beauty of the world for her and her daughter to enjoy.

The road leading to the property curved for miles without any crossings. Very few people outside of residence traveled on the narrow dirt road. Shannon had no particular destination in mind as she moved along the peaceful road, listening to the birds singing and feeling the gentle wind caress her skin. It was a beautiful day.

"Hello, young lady," a soft voice says from behind.

Surprised to hear anyone on what Shannon knew to be an unpopulated road, she turned to see an old woman whose face and body have been molded by time. "Hello," she responded, "it's a lovely day for a stroll, isn't it?"

"Yes, yes, it is a very lovely day; too lovely to be inside. When I was your age, nothing could keep me inside on a day like this. As soon as I got the chance I would gallivant and stay out as long as the sun was out. I guess I still have that bug in me. I just don't move as well anymore. Do you mind if I travel with you young lady? I won't slow you up too much."

"Oh, it's no problem with me, Ma'am."

"Please, call me Sheryl. "Ma'am" makes me feel old."

"I'm sorry, how rude of me. I'm Shannon."

"That's a lovely name. I had a friend named Shannon when I was in elementary school. She was a nice girl and we always had a lot of fun together, but she moved away suddenly. We weren't even able to say goodbye. That was a long time ago."

"Did you ever find out what became of her?"

"No, I never heard any more about her. Not even rumors. Life is like that sometimes, the things that we truly want are the things that sometimes are never meant to happen. I guess that's what drives our purpose, the yearning to be more. Without that, life would be pretty boring, huh?"

Shannon replied smiling, "Yeah, I suppose it would... Sheryl?"

"Yes, Shannon?"

"Since your old friend hasn't returned yet, I would like to become your new friend. I'll be your new Shannon. Would that be ok?"

The old woman smiled infectiously. "I would be honored to accept your friendship Shannon. I'm an old woman who has outlived many in her lifetime. Company is something that has become of great value to me. Your friendship couldn't have come at a better time. Now, shall we enjoy this day together?"

"Yes, let's. Where are we headed, Sheryl?"

"There's a garage sale up the road. Old man Kelly runs it on the third Saturday of every month. He's a nice man and he's been all over the world. He was famous at one time for his art, but he shunned the fame and moved here with his family. A truck from the city comes in once a month and drops off things from his old life. Such virtue in a wealthy man who shuns greed and wastefulness. I think you will like him." Shannon took Sheryl's extended hand in hers and the two women traveled on to the garage sale.

Old man Kelly's estate was massive. The property extended as far as the eye could see. It was a beautifully manicured landscape with all sorts of workings and happenings: a farm, a winery, a ranch, a school, and several living quarters scattered around the estate. In her mind Shannon had pictured a small garage sale when she was told where they were headed, but what she saw did not fit her idea of a garage sale. It was more like a flea market, with music, food, games and people everywhere enjoying the company of the day, buying and selling goods on the lush grass of the estate.

Sheryl led Shannon through the market. The old woman turned into a young girl right before Shannon's eyes. No longer did she move slowly, nor did she seem feeble or tired; she was vibrant and full of life. They came to a booth containing several beautiful paintings. An old man with brown skin, a lean, shaved head and face who sat writing on paper in the back of the booth didn't look up as he greeted them,

"Hello Sheryl! It's good to see you. Who's your friend?"

Sheryl beamed with excitement upon hearing the man's voice. "Oh, this is my friend Shannon. She's new. This is her first time to the market."

"Please come in and have a seat." The man said, still looking down. The two women went inside the booth and sat. Shannon chose a rocking chair that squeaked with age. The man finally looked up from his writing. "What can I do for you and your friend, Sheryl?"

"Well I'm fine, but my friend here needs something from the market. She needs something to call her own."

"I see, I see," the man said turning his eyes toward Shannon. "Let me ask you a question, young lady. If enough people believe something does it give that something more power?"

"Well, things do increase in power as more people believe in them."

"Then it is safe to say that one person's belief in something is just as relevant as a million others?"

Shannon thought for a moment before answering. "Well, even if a million people believe differently than one person, that one person's belief could be powerful enough to pose a challenge to the masses, and so that one person could change the minds of many; some would call that a revolution."

The old man laughed approvingly. "You are a very wise young woman, not many are able to understand this power, the power of one. Give me something of value."

Shannon looked at him quizzically. "What do you mean?"

The old man remained silent, only extending an open hand. Shannon remembered she had a few dollars in her pocket. She retrieved them and placed the bills in the old man's hand. He smiled at her as he pulled out a lighter and set fire to the money. As the bills burned he dropped them onto a dish saying, "That has no value here."

Sheryl laughed. "I'm sorry Shannon; I forgot to tell you money is worthless here."

The old man stared at the burning money and extended his palm. "Just because a million people believe something, does not make that something true. My power as one man states this fact against a billion who oppose it. Give me something of value."

Having no jewelry and money being no good here, Shannon found herself at a loss. All she could do was take the old man's hand in hers and say, "Sir, the only thing I have of value is myself. That is my most valued asset. For without this I have nothing. I will share this most valued possession with you, in friendship, if you will accept."

The old man's eyes seemed to look right though her, as if they could see deep into her heart. He smiled warmly, "I accept your gift. I will be your friend, young Shannon. I want you to take the chair you are seated in home. Put it in a place that the world can see, and the peace of life shall be yours. I must return to my work, please feel free to come here whenever you want. It's open to you my friend. Go in peace."

When the two women emerged from the booth carrying the rocking chair, a tall, slender, freckle faced man walked up to them smiling. "Hey Sheryl! Where you headed?" He gestured to take the chair from them.

"We're headed to my friend's house. She's the wife of the new Reverend."

Shannon looked at her with surprise. Sheryl winked and whispered, "I was your friend before you ever met me."

That evening sitting in her rocking chair and entertaining her new friend in the living room, Shannon felt the peace Mr. Kelly spoke of. When the Reverend came into the house he quickly scurried into his room with young Rio for bible study. He said his hello's and made his escape very quickly. A few weeks passed like this with the two women meeting and enjoying their time together in the living room. The Reverend knew he could not be cold to Shannon in front of Sheryl, one of his new parishioners, so to put on a good show, he fixed up the guest room and put Shannon's things in there. She continued entertaining Sheryl in the living room. The house was hers.

The day of Sheryl's funeral was cold. Shannon couldn't remember a colder day. After spending many years together, Sheryl had come to understand the ways of Shannon's home. The Reverend always kept Rio close to him, and not once in all the women's years together did Rio spend time with them. For years Sheryl watched this strange relationship. She never inquired about it, rather she ignored it as though it was not taking place. Finally, on Rio's thirteenth birthday Sheryl made Shannon promise that she would send Rio out into the world to find love.

Watching them lower Sheryl into her grave Shannon vowed again to keep her promise. Only six months had passed since Sheryl's request and now here they were. Maybe Sheryl knew that her time was almost over. Whatever the case, Shannon missed her a great deal. The time she spent with Sheryl was the longest she had spent with any friend.

The Reverend continued his methods of keeping Rio away from Shannon. When Shannon took control of the house, the Reverend tightened his grip on Rio by taking her to the church every morning, only returning for supper, eating in silence, then retiring to the Reverend's room for bible study before going to sleep, and beginning the routine all over again the next day.

Rio had developed an interest in drawing, and she could be found with a sketch pad or a paint brush whenever she could find time. For her fourteenth birthday the Reverend allowed Rio to paint outside. He'd finally changed his routine and Shannon did not let this opportunity pass without taking advantage of it.

One Sunday after church the Reverend was distracted by some of his new parishioners and missed Shannon walking down the path toward the church. Painting outside and consumed by her work, Rio didn't see her either. Shannon's heart fluttered as she approached her beautiful daughter.

"Hello Rio," she said in a soft, motherly tone.

The young girl turned to her and smiled but didn't say anything, making her reason clear by directing her eyes toward the church.

"Don't worry about The Reverend, Rio. He cannot see us right now. Old man Kelly is talking to him about the ways of man. They should be awhile."

Rio looked back toward her painting, continuing where she left off.

"It's okay Rio, you do not have to talk. I came to you. I just want you to hear my voice. We have not been allowed to speak to each other since you were born, and when we did speak it wasn't much of a conversation, but I want you to know that I have always loved you and I will not let the Reverend stand in our way any longer. One day we are going to leave here and go to some place beautiful. I'm your mother, Rio, and I will never leave you alone.

The young girl's paint strokes stopped on the canvas. She turned around and smiled.

"That's right," Shannon said, "Mommy's little angel is going to be happy someday soon. I must go my love. I'll talk to you again. Keep painting. Your work is beautiful just like you."

Shannon walked away with tears of both triumph and sorrow, having no idea when she would speak to her daughter again but knowing somehow, she would.

Many days passed into months, which formed a year of Shannon secretly meeting with Rio. Their conversations were nothing more than passing words or gestures; three to four sentences before being out of ear shot and having to wait until the next opportunity to do it again. The two developed this method so that Shannon could speak to another person in front of Rio and deliver a message directly to her daughter. Even words spoken under her breath became parts of unfinished conversations and the seeds planted began to take root.

Rio began to rebel, defying some of the Reverend's requests, questioning his commands, and objecting to his desires. He would never punish Rio in front of Shannon, but once they were alone, he punished her worse than any chastisement. She knew what he was doing. Rio was a beautiful young girl whose budding body was not hard to notice. Shannon checked the Reverend's sheets and found all the proof she needed. She begged Rio to sleep in the living room where she could watch and make sure her little girl was safe. For a while it ensured that Rio would have a good night's rest, but the Reverend's would find ways to be alone with the young girl. Shannon had enough and decided it was time to end this battle. She told Rio to run away to a place that she has only seen in a dream, a park filled with kind people who would care for her. Shannon knew Shadow was there and that he would make sure Rio found him. Rio trusted her mother's vision and left in the middle of the night, looking for a place called People's Park.

Shannon worried while Rio was gone. Her heart grew heavier with each day during her daughter's absence. She'd given her money for a start, but as a mother she knew her daughter was vulnerable to so many things, having never seen the outside world before. This small scratch of land had been her entire world. No television, radios, or computers to encounter the daily events of outside life.

Nine months had passed by when Shannon started to lose hope for her daughter's return. Shannon wondered if the dream had been a vision or delusional desires. While hanging laundry on the clothes lines outside, tears fell from her eyes. The curse had claimed another victim. In her attempt to break it, it reared its ugly face in opposition to claim the one last thing she lived for. She'd done her best to disguise her love for the young girl because she knew loving her only brought harm, but her weakness caused by the strength of her desires allowed the curse to strike again. There was nothing left to live for now that Rio was free. It was all for the best.

"Mom." Shannon jumped. It couldn't be. "Mom." From behind her the sweet melodic voice, she'd been wishing for. "I'm home

Mom."

Shannon was almost too afraid to move for fear it couldn't be real. She turned to see her beautiful little girl. Laundry to be hung still in hand, she embraced her daughter for the first time, the joy in her heart radiating all the moments she had missed.

"Rio! I missed you so much. Are you alright, honey? Did everything go okay?" She asked, pulling back a bit so she could examine her little girl's face.

"Yes Mom, everything is fine. I'm fine. Nothing bad happened to me."

"You were gone for so long, honey. I began to doubt if you would ever come home."

Rio sighed deeply. "Mom, this is not my home, and this is not your home. I didn't want to come back here, but I couldn't bear the thought of leaving you behind."

"Oh Rio, I'm fine honey. As long as you're happy I'll always be fine."

"I know, Mom, I know. I have a message for you from Shadow."
Shannon was relieved.

The Reverend returned from church to find Rio had come home. He displayed no emotional reaction whatsoever, acting as if she never left. He walked inside, said hello, and ate his dinner but before saying goodnight and retiring to his room, he asked Rio if she would accompany him to the church in the morning. She answered no, saying she refused to attend church until the Reverend allowed her to go to a public school. After months of resistance, he finally agreed to let her go.

It had been a short three years since Shannon made her promise to Sheryl, and Rio was now out of the house attending school. She was outside looking for love, looking for the king whose love could save her from the Reverend. Shannon watched and waited every night for Rio to come home and speak about love and of loving someone.

Finally, the name of a young boy, Ethan, crossed her daughter's lips, with a familiar melody of sound.

Listening to Rio's song of Ethan, Shannon knew it wouldn't be long before the curse would strike again. Shannon would see that the curse would end with Rio. She told her daughter that if she refused the young boy in an abrupt fashion he would free her from the Reverend. With a pit in her stomach and pain in her heart knowing what Rio would soon endure, Shannon told Rio to return home every day before the sun goes down, and not to refuse the Reverend. Rio did as her mother instructed.

The night Shannon decided to pray at the church and not to watch her daughter come home was the night the Reverend died. After the lights from the police cars and futile ambulances had faded, the two women sat alone in the house staring at the blood pooled on the living room floor. Rio felt the weight of the curse her mother had warned her about. She had loved the young boy who rode his roaring white horse to save her, and now the curse had stolen him from her. Shannon felt the curse had been satisfied, at least in this newly lost love, but she knew it hadn't been broken.

"Mom?" Rio broke the silence.

"Yes, honey?"

"I – I - I want to leave here. Can we please go? Please?"

Shannon sighed, reminded that the curse must be fed once more. "It is not time yet, and there is something I must tell you."

"What? What is it Mom?"

Shannon shivered in her rocking chair. "You have a father and a sister who are both living near each other but don't know each other."

"What? Mom? What are you saying?"

The rocking chair creaked as a tear trickled from Shannon's left eye.

"The Reverend was an evil, evil man and he lied to you. Now I'm going to tell you about your father."

Shannon told Rio all about her father, Charles, and how the

Reverend stole her older sister Eva and put her up for adoption. The story wrenched Rio's heart; her father had abandoned her. Shannon tells Rio what needs be done to break the curse. She cringed at the thought but felt the truth of her mother's words reverberate deep within her. In the morning Rio set out to find them. She knew it was her and her alone who could bring her sister the peace she needed, and her father, his revelation.

It had been almost a year since she'd left. Rio knew her love was cursed, and she knew that her father and sister would love her. Shannon smiled in her rocking chair, thinking about how Eva and Charles lived only a few miles apart and had no idea they were related. It was funny to her how life had kept them close to each other.

Charles was a cold, selfish man who needed to feel his youngest daughter's touch of love. Eva was a very sick young girl taken unjustly from the love of her family; she deserved to meet the man who had brought her into this world. Silently, Shannon prayed, rocking in her chair.

Tap, tap against the window. *Tap, tap* against the window again. The moon was full, and Shannon was reminded of the times when she was a young girl with Claudia and they traveled in the light of darkness. She got up and opened the door to see that Rio was home. Shannon's heart burst wide open feeling all the love she'd tried to keep safely locked up. She knew what had been done and tears of release and joy ran down Shannon's face. The curse had been broken.

"Mom, Shadow awaits us. We seek no more."

Shannon placed a handmade flower wreath on Rio's crown and hugged her tightly. "I love you honey, I love you so much. You ready?"

"Yes, Mom, I'm ready."

"Take my hand, the light of darkness awaits us."

The two women walked out into the night. Their path glowed under the moonlight. Rio's love had brought them to the crossing of their parallel paths. Together, their paths crossed into shadow as one, they entered with their hands clasped together. When they reached the place where the street met the forest, in the distance they could see Shadow getting closer to their reflection.

"Your seeking is complete young Shannon. You both shall enjoy love without fear of losing its presence. The path of love is a road revealed through living desire. Individuals can travel next to it without ever knowing it is truly there. The reflection of love grants access to the being. Love seeks only to recognize the eternal connection of two or more existing. Those in love with their individual journey are cursed to never see their own reflection, and those in love with their individual journey will only see themselves in pieces, like a broken mirror."

Shannon and Rio knelt and closed their eyes in the great Shadow's presence.

"Thank you, wise Shadow for showing us the way."

Shannon opened her eyes to find herself alone in front of the mirror, kneeling in prayer.

"Mom," Rio enters her bedroom, "we need to go to Old Man Kelly's before the truck leaves. Last time we missed it."

Rio stood behind Shannon in the mirror. Their image together caused Shannon to reflect on the last time she looked in a mirror. But this time the mirror didn't shatter. It merely reflected the eternal commitment of love with no fear of losing love's presence. For them love was no longer a fantasy.

www.ingramcontent.com/pod-product-compliance
Lightning Source LLC
Chambersburg PA
CBHW051923240626
47153CB00004B/1337